THE WINNING TICKET

REVISED EDITION

A NOVEL

CARROLL MULTZ

AUTHOR OF
DEADLY DECEPTION

The Winning Ticket

Revised Edition
Copyright © 2023, 2017
by Carroll Multz

Published by
ShahrazaD Publishing®
2189 W Canyon Court
Grand Junction, CO 81507

Library of Congress Control Number: 2023906658

ISBN – 979889034584-4

Visit the author at: carrollmultz@charter.net

Also by Carroll Multz

Adult Novels

Justice Denied • *Deadly Deception* • *License to Convict*

The Devil's Scribe • *The Chameleon*

Shades of Innocence • *The Winning Ticket (First Edition)*

with Judith Blevins

Rogue Justice • *The Plagiarist (First Edition)* • *A Desperate Plea*

Spiderweb • *The Méjico Connection* • *Eyewitness* • *Lust for Revenge*

Kamanda • *Bloodline* • *Pickpocket* • *Ghost Writer* • *Guilt by Innuendo*

Gypsy Card Reader • *Waves of Vengeance* • *Veil of Deceit*

The Journalist • *We the Jury* • *Star Chamber* • *Reflection of a Killer*

Bonsai • *The Gemini Connection* • *Stille Nacht*

The Plagiarist (Second Edition) • *Déjà Vu* • *Undue Influence* • *Sabenia*

Childhood Legends Series® with Judith Blevins

Operation Cat Tale • *One Frightful Day* • *Blue*

The Ghost of Bradbury Mansion • *White Out*

Flash of Red • *Back in Time* • *Treasure Seekers*

Summer Vacation-Part 1: Castaways-Part 2: Blast Off

A Trip to Remember — The R*U*1*2s Journey to the Nation's Capital

A series of novels for middle-grade readers

*This novel is dedicated
to my mother and father
who taught me a love for music
and a zest for life.*

What passion

cannot

music raise

and quell?

DRYDEN

TABLE OF CONTENTS

I was raised in a musical family and learned early on that music was the foretaste of our heavenly kingdom. With my mother's voice and the way my father tickled the ivories on his accordion and the family piano, I knew I was destined to make music an integral part of my life. I'd be remiss if I did not mention the star in our musical family—my sister, Marilynn—who played the clarinet as well as the piano and was a member of the orchestra at our high school and a member of the marching band. Her dedication and determination wore off on me. Without her, I'd still be playing the piano with one finger.

I took classical piano lessons starting at age ten and by high school was playing the contemporary songs of the day. Growing up in the West, I kept secret my musical side for the better part of my youth, especially my tap dancing on stage with my sister as a preschooler. With a name like Carroll (even with two r's and two l's), I learned to be rough and tumble in order to survive. My classmates and neighborhood pals were brutal. It was fight or flight!

It wasn't until I collaborated with composer Ed Rogers in 1970 on a song we called *Don't Give Me Tomorrow*, that I began to record some of my musical compositions. *Don't Give Me Tomorrow* was played to a bossa nova rhythm at the Penrose Room of the famous Broadmoor Hotel in Colorado Springs, Colorado, and provided the impetus for my subsequent compositions.

Combining my music with many of my novels has become commonplace starting with *Deadly Deception* and culminating with *The Winning Ticket*. Music, like my novels, is intended to inspire, inform and entertain. Hopefully, you will find the blend in the novel you are about to read a memorable one.

I express my gratitude to Judith Blevins, Gary Smith and Julie Jacobson whose musical talents contributed greatly in making this novel what it is and to Jan Weeks, Margie Vollmer Rabdau, and my book designer, Frank Addington, for their technical assistance. And last but not least, my gratitude to Rosalie Stewart and John Lukon of KC Book Manufacturing for printing the revised edition of The Winning Ticket.

———

PROLOGUE

"Damn it, Ashley, answer the phone," Brad ordered, as he angrily folded the morning newspaper and tossed it onto the table.

Ashley picked up the phone and glanced at the caller ID. "It's you know who," she said.

Brad folded his arms across his chest in a display of disgust, and replied, "Of course I know who it is, but are you just gonna let the phone ring all day?"

"Brad, I don't want to encourage Grady. You know how I feel about the bastard," Ashley snapped, pouring herself another cup of coffee. Then, looking at Brad, she held up the carafe.

Brad shook his head, "Thanks, but I've had enough caffeine and enough of Grady to last a lifetime!"

"You're not alone!" Ashley responded. Then she added, "Maybe it's about Shelly or Sherry."

"Regardless, you know how persistent your ex is. He'll hound you as long as his heart is pounding, not only to get you to respond but to win you back."

"I've thought about that," Ashley said. "Even divorce and ignoring him hasn't worked. If it weren't for our joint business dealings, the court would have granted my repeated requests for restraining orders and he wouldn't be the pest that he is." Then Ashley sighed. "Guess I have no choice. When he calls again I'll answer."

• • •

Ashley grabbed the phone on its first ring. "What do you want this time? Never mind. To save us both some time and to cut to thechase my answer is an unequivocal no."

"Maybe when you hear what I have to say, dear heart," Grady responded, "you won't be so quick to turn your back on me."

"Don't tell me your Uncle Cordell finally croaked and you inherited his fortune?" Ashley said, rolling her eyes.

"Something much better," Grady said in an authoritative tone.

"I give up!" Ashley sighed. "What could be better than inheriting your uncle's estate?"

"Winning the lottery," Grady replied.

Laughingly, Ashley said, "Sure, and I hope you use some of your winnings to book a room at the loony bin." Then after a pause, she added, "Sounds to me like you're back on the sauce."

Grady said, "Ashley, you know I still love you and want you back."

"Not gonna happen in this lifetime. I gave you plenty of chances. Even after the divorce I was willing to reconcile our differences and get back together," Ashley retorted.

Grady's sigh came clearly over the phone. "That was then, this is now. I was different when I left and now I'm not the same. Give me a chance to prove my love."

"Where've I heard that before?" Ashley said more as a statement than a question.

After a long pause, Grady said, "I wouldn't lie to you. And as far as my drinking days are concerned, I have been sober now for a number of years."

Out of the corner of her eye, Ashley noticed Brad making motions with his hands indicating for her to hurry up and end the call. Ashley ignored him. "The road to hell is paved with good intentions. I wouldn't believe what you told me even if you swore on a stack of Bibles."

Grady, in a contrite voice, said, "I know I had my chance and that my track record isn't great but this time, I swear, I've hit the mother lode."

Ashley looked at Brad and rolled her eyes. She then asked Grady, "How often have you told me that? Let me count the times—"

"Okay, I know, I know. But, this time, I assure you, I'm telling the truth and my motives are honorable. It's about you, me and the lottery."

"Grady," Ashley said, "it's no longer about you and me so let's not go into that. I'm not interested in reconciling—not now or ever!"

"Even if I've won the PowerBall jackpot?" Grady said, and it sounded more like a plea than a question.

"Not even then," Ashley responded. Then, stringing him along, she asked, "How much did you allegedly win?"

"One point five billion."

Ashley put her hand over the mouthpiece and yelled at Brad, "Guess what? Wink, wink, according to Grady, he just won the one point five billion dollar PowerBall jackpot." Brad was immediately at Ashley's side signaling that he wanted the phone. Ashley shook her head and moved away still holding the phone.

Clutching the phone, Ashley said, "Grady, that's the best one yet. Your imagination is certainly working overtime...at least something is working."

"Let me have the damn phone," Brad demanded. Grabbing the phone, Brad said, "Grady, why don't you just give it up and get used to the idea that you're the odd man out? You're ancient history as far as Ashley is concerned. When are you going to get it through your thick skull that I'm the winner? I'm the man Ashley has always dreamed of and wants to be with."

"You're as big a gold digger as she is," Grady said. "Put Ashley back on the phone. I don't have the time or the energy to make this a marathon."

Ashley said, when she came back on the phone, "Excuse the interruption." Then, in a much softer voice, she asked, "How do you know you've won the lottery?"

"I've checked the numbers." His voice rose. "They match. I'm the big winner."

"You may have to share with other winners," Ashley said.

Grady rushed on. "If there are two other winners, then I've only won a cool half billion."

"What are your numbers?"

"You sound as if you don't believe me. Go ahead, see for yourself, check page seven in today's newspaper. The winning numbers mirror mine, or should I say mine mirror theirs."

"Hold on," Ashley said as she reached for the paper Brad had tossed on the table.

As Ashley searched for the right page, she was stymied in her attempt by Brad's interference. As she fumbled in her futile attempt to find the section with the desired information, Brad grabbed the paper from her and wadded it up and tossed it into the wastepaper basket.

Ashley folded her arms across her chest and glared at Brad. "Why'd you do that?" she asked.

Brad replied, "Don't waste your time on that knucklehead. He'll say or do anything to get your attention."

When Ashley came back on the line, she asked with unexpected civility, "Grady, can I call you back?"

"Of course," Grady answered.

• • •

After Grady hung up the phone, he felt more than a glimmer of hope. If nothing more, at least I've piqued her curiosity, he thought. He then retrieved an old family photo of Ashley, the twins and himself and kissed it reverently. Shelly and Sherry were just babies at the time. Now they were in their early twenties and living on their own.

As he waited for Ashley to call back, he paced back and forth. Occasionally, he would look in the direction of the phone. It was over three hours since he had spoken to her and he was beginning to feel as though he had been sandbagged, or more aptly, stood up. When it came to Ashley, that kind of thing was not only anticipated but expected. He thought he should have known better.

Grady jammed his hands in his pants pockets and was on the verge of giving up when the telephone rang.

He checked caller ID. As he hoped, it was Ashley. "Hello?" he answered.

"Okay, we can talk now," Ashley said in a tone reminiscent of the days before their quarrelsome separation and divorce. "Brad can be a distraction, you know. Now, where were we?"

"Did you check the numbers in the newspaper?" Grady asked.

"Yeah! What are yours?" Ashley replied.

Grady speculated that once she checked the numbers, she'd want to see the ticket itself. Doubting Thomas! She's friendly only when she thinks it might benefit her. Otherwise, she will use me, and when she's through with me, throw me away like an old newspaper. Perhaps, I should think this through.

"Well, then?" Ashley said with agitation in her voice.

After a pause, Grady said, "two, sixteen, fifty-two, fifty-four and fifty-six. The PowerPlay number is thirteen." Grady had deliberately given her wrong numbers. She'd be calling right back. If she were livid, he'd write reconciliation off as a lost cause. If she was the Ashley he had fallen in love with, he'd give her the correct numbers and let nature take its course.

• • •

Grady had barely hung up when the phone rang. Before Grady could say, "Hello?" Ashley blurted, "You conniving bastard! You had me convinced you were telling the truth. It never fails. Every time I let my guard down, you take advantage of me. When will I ever learn?" Grady could hear whispering. Ashley was no doubt conferring with Brad.

Returning, she asked, "Well, what do you have to say for yourself?"

"I gave you the wrong numbers on purpose. I wanted to test your reaction to see if your sudden change of attitude toward me was because you wanted a share of the winnings or because of your feelings for me. Guess I got my answer. I suppose it's my turn to ask, 'When will I ever learn?'"

"Go back to your numb juice and feed your fantasies and retreat to your dream world. Only this time leave me out! You're a loser, always have been and always will be. The only thing you've won is the proof that you are the worthless bum I knew from the start."

Grady could hear Ashley's and Brad's laughter as he hung up. This time, he thought, he'd have the last laugh.

• • •

Curious as to what the tax consequences would be on a one point five-billion-dollar jackpot, the next day Grady called his accountant, Willard Dean.

"Will, Grady Winslow here," Grady said, as he rummaged around his desk looking for a pen and pad so he could record the information he was seeking from Will.

"Grady, haven't heard from you for a while. What can I do for you?"

"I was curious about what tax the winner of the one point five-billion-dollar PowerBall jackpot would have to pay. I have a bet with a poker buddy that the takeaway will be in the neighborhood of a billion dollars. My buddy claims it would be more like three quarters of a billion." Grady paused, then asked, "Which one of us is the closest?"

"Grady, you old dog. Don't tell me you purchased the winning ticket?" Will asked.

"Ha! If that were the case, I'd be booking a world cruise, not phoning you. We were just curious."

"Ouch! That hurts!" Will bellowed and then said, "Give me a minute." Grady could hear the noise of a calculator being activated. "If it's a cash lump sum and the jackpot is a cool one point five billion as reported, the proceeds would be taxed by the feds at thirty-nine point six percent which comes to… five hundred ninety-four million." More sounds as the calculator was led through its paces. "The Colorado tax would be thirty-seven million. The combined taxes would be… six hundred thirty-one million. One point five billion or one thousand five hundred million minus six hundred thirty-one million comes out to… eight hundred sixty-nine million."

Grady did some quick calculations of his own. "Looks like my buddy was only off by one hundred and nineteen million; I was off by a whopping one hundred and thirty-one million. Guess he was the closest. Then again, what's twelve million among friends? Thanks for the information."

"Sure. That was a good diversion and a chance to rest my eyes. I've never had occasion to calculate taxes on that much moola. Hope your wager with your poker buddy wasn't for more than a few dollars," Will said, as he appeared to be checking Grady's calculations. "I'll keep the figures handy just in case."

If only you knew! Grady thought.

• • •

After a fitful night's sleep, Grady awoke with an epiphany as to what he should do in light of his recent rejection by Ashley —a rejection he vowed, if he had his way, would be the last. He showered and dressed. He placed the page of the newspaper with the winning numbers and his winning lottery ticket in an envelope and sealed it. He addressed the envelope to Ashley. He then drove to his lawyer's office.

When he reached the law offices of Chevalier, Mills & Greenberg, he asked the receptionist if he could speak to Adison Chevalier.

"I'm sorry, Mr. Chevalier is in with a client at the moment and is booked for the rest of the day," Thelma, the receptionist, said as she thumbed through a day planner. "The earliest we can schedule you is Monday of next week at ten a.m." She looked up from the appointment book, "Would that work?"

"Can I just leave this for him?" Grady asked, waiving the sealed envelope.

"Of course," Thelma replied as she reached for it. "I'll give this to Mr. Chevalier's secretary for safekeeping. She'll know what to do with it."

Grady was hesitant to just leave the envelope containing, in essence, one point five billion dollars. After a moment of reflection, he asked, "Since I can't speak to Mr. Chevalier in person, perhaps I should write the instructions on the envelope. May I borrow a pen?"

"Yes, of course." She handed Grady a pen. He began scribbling on the envelope, and when he had finished, he handed the pen and envelope back. "If Mr. Chevalier has any questions or is unsure about the instructions, have him call me."

"Of course. Is it okay if I stamp today's date on the envelope?"

"That would be fine."

· · ·

At home, Grady looked through old photo albums. There were several loose photographs at the front of the album which Grady examined first. A tattered wallet-size photograph of Ashley caught his eye. He fingered it tenderly and tears formed. He wondered how many years he carried the photo in his wallet. It was given to him by Ashley when they first met. It literally traveled with him the full breadth of this planet. If only he had responded to her beck and call, he wouldn't be pursuing her today.

CHAPTER ONE

The Prelude

GRADY

My mother leans out the window and shouts, "Charlie, must you and Freddie throw the ball against the house? Can't you find some other place to play while Grady practices his piano?"

"When will he be through?" Charlie asks impatiently.

"We've been waiting for what seems like hours," Freddie says as he throws his bat and glove down and defiantly folds his arms across his chest.

"Patience, lads. Grady still has another twenty minutes and then he'll be out," Mom says.

"Yeah!" Charlie says, kicking at a clump of dirt. "We'll be timing ya."

I listen to the exchange but keep playing so that I won't have to start from the beginning.

Mom pulls her head back in and scolds, "Wrong note!" I nod and continue to bang away.

• • •

I grew up in New York City and spent a good part of my youth travelling literally all over the world. My father was a concert pianist and my mother a recording artist. My father was the third in a line of concert pianists. Graden Winslow was a household name back in the day. My mother went by her maiden name Bella Ramey. Her father was third in a line of medical doctors.

"How can you play all that stilted music?" my mother would complain to my father.

Not to be outdone in the insult department, my father would

reply, "How can you sing lyrics that are pure nonsense?"

I kept silent, but in my heart, I agreed with Mom. Needless to say, I found classical music humdrum and featureless, at least back then. Because of my lack of interest and inability to remember the complex combination of notes, I would improvise. I could create sounds that were pleasing and more moving than the classical jumble of sounds.

I remember vividly the day that I wanted to trade classical music for contemporary or popular music and made the announcement to my parents. In order to show them I was serious, I then sat down and played a perfect rendition of *Don't Worry, Be Happy* that I had memorized at a friend's house. My parents were speechless. I then played *Livin' on a Prayer.* Dad just glared at me.

"How is it Grady can't play classical without the sheet music and yet can play flawless contemporary music without so much as a cue?" my father asked my mother, obviously disgusted.

"No doubt a sign of discerning taste and an appreciation for sounds that tickle the ears," Mom replied. "Shouldn't he play music he enjoys?"

"He would be disregarding a legacy established by his father, grandfather and great grandfather," Dad said as he pointed a rigid forefinger to the wall above the fireplace that was lined with photographs of three generations of concert pianists. "We deliberately left a fourth spot vacant for you," he said and looked at me as if I were a traitor. Although I felt guilty and Dad was good at eliciting guilt, I was stubbornly determined to make my own way.

I was a junior in high school and had always been taught by both of my parents that I was not a clone and that I should make careful decisions based on my own better judgment. When I reminded Dad of his sage advice, he nodded.

"Dad, I could never be the pianist that you are. If I could and did succeed, it would be because of you. If I failed, it would be despite you. In either case, it would be you and not me. I want to be my own person and a blend of both you and Mom."

I'll never forget Dad leaning forward on his crossed arms and saying, "You are our whole life, son. You are our only heir. It's obvious you inherited the music traits from both sides of the family. How you use your talents are between you as the beneficiary and our God as the benefactor." Then Dad looked at me and raised his brow. "Remember, to him who is given much, much is expected."

It was only a matter of days after our heart-to-heart talk that Charlie, Freddie, Jimmy, Danny and I formed The New York Five, a band, at least in our eyes, that was rivaled only by the Beatles. Charlie and Freddie played guitars, Jimmy, the drums, Danny, the sax and me. I was the keyboardist and leader of the band. Our theme song was a number I wrote called *Right Frame of Mind*.

From the days of my early childhood, I was obsessed with music. I heard heavenly sounds while I slept that, as I grew older, I would play on the piano. It wasn't long before I recorded them on a tape recorder and later used letters of the notes to record them on sheet music. Everything early on was in the key of C. It was only after a series of piano lessons that I began penning notes. I had resisted the traditional chords to complement my right hand and opted instead to create my own chords or combination of notes.

That I was on the right track was confirmed by a music teacher who told me my chords were so beautiful they brought tears to her eyes. Whether exaggeration or not, I continued to improvise and experiment with various renditions until I was satisfied with the sound. Ms. Brazelton was the first one who allowed me to vary from the script and do my own arrangements. My mother later relented and allowed me the same latitude provided the sounds were sweet.

Although I was a good athlete and enjoyed sports, my mind was mainly on music. Even during grade school and high school, I found it difficult to concentrate. My mind was preoccupied by music and writing. When I wasn't playing or writing music, I was writing poems and short stories. I was given a D in deportment by my sixth-grade teacher because she tired of scolding me and confiscating my "diversions."

ASHLEY

My name is Tamara Ashley Harden, but I go by Ashley. I'm a sophomore at Central High School in Grand Junction, Colorado. I'm a member of the CHS chorale and theatre troupes as well as the CHS band. I've been taking clarinet, piano and voice lessons since fifth grade. My father is a second-generation medical doctor, my mother a music teacher at Central. She also sings in the church choir at Shepherd of the Valley Lutheran Church.

My second year of high school is challenging, and like the first, consists mainly of basic courses. My favorite course is music appreciation. My grandfather on my mother's side was a music composer and wrote a number of songs for national performers. Although he and my grandmother live in the Denver area, we spend a lot of time together. Being their only grandchild, I receive a lot of attention.

I feel as though I'm caught in the middle. My father wants me to follow in his footsteps and become an M.D. My grandfather, on the other hand, wants me to become a music composer and go to CSU in Ft. Collins after high school. I must admit science is not my forte and that my passion is music. When I tell my father this, he tells me to keep an open mind. "If you find you like biology and chemistry, you may want to change your mind and pursue a career in medicine." Mom, on the other hand, wants me to follow my dreams.

GRADY

"Grady," Mom calls, "dinner is ready. Come on, son, you know how Dad hates to be kept waiting."

I'm in my room studying for finals. My senior year is coming to an end and I'm still battling my parents over what university to attend. This evening during dinner, we have a pretty heated conversation.

"But I don't want to go to Juilliard," I say, "I hate classical music."

"Music is music," Dad says, as he gently places his fork on his dinner plate and reaches for his glass of wine. "Juilliard is considered the most prestigious music conservatory in the country. Besides, your grandfather helped endow the school."

"Grady, at Julliard, it's not just about classical music," Mom interjects. "Their programs are designed to prepare students for careers in the contemporary music industry as well. Read their brochure and see for yourself."

I love my parents but they have a way of laying the old guilt trip on me whenever I disagree with them. "I believe you, Mom. But they accept less than twenty percent of those who apply. Whose to say I'll even be accepted?"

"You have the talent and the grades," Dad assures me. "Besides, both your father and grandfather are alums."

Guilt, guilt, guilt. Alums. Who cares this day and age? "But Charlie and Freddie are going to Farleigh College of Music in Boston," I counter.

"I thought you were the leader of the band," Dad says. "Since when has a kid of mine been a follower?" He shakes his head, apparently in disgust.

"Farleigh has a great program," Mom interjects. *What's this? Is Mom really on my side?*

"So do about twenty others," Dad says. "Why not just stay in New York and be close to home?" His eyes probe mine. I look away.

"But Grady is more interested in getting out from under our thumbs," Mom says. "Since Grady's focus is on contemporary, as opposed to classical music, Farleigh is an ideal choice. Besides, Boston is really not that far from home."

Sounds like Mom has taken up my cause in earnest. However, in true fashion, Dad doesn't give up easily.

"If he goes to Farleigh, he'll be a small fish in a big pond. He has a better chance at making his mark if he goes to Juilliard. I'd even rather see him go to Manhattan School of Music."

ASHLEY

"Hey, Ashley, come on. We're skipping the cafeteria and going out for pizza," Theresa Redkin coaxes, as she passes my locker. I'm a junior at Central now and have become a jazz pianist. I've become quite the celebrity by playing several of my own compositions. Grandfather Holliday is proud of me and has offered to pay my tuition, board and room if I become a music major and attend CSU. My father has made the same offer if I become a pre-med major. He's relented a little and admitted I have a future in the music world.

"There is still over a year left of high school," he says and crosses his fingers. "Maybe you'll get religion and realize that there is a greater calling in serving others."

Arguing with Dad is as useless as arguing with a judge—no matter how good your case, you just can't win. However, I inherited some of Dad's spunk and I, too, refuse to concede. "Entertaining is just as healing as operations and pills," I say. "In fact, music has been found to have a therapeutic effect."

"Okay then, next time you have a broken arm, call a musician." Dad smirks.

"It's probably cheaper and more effective," I respond.

"And a lot less risky." Mom's comment takes the edge off the situation. We all laugh.

GRADY

It is 1981 and graduation is a blast. Our band, The New York Five, plays at the reception that follows. Parents, relatives and friends, including mine, are in attendance. We are playing the greatest hits of the '70s and I'm moved as I watch my parents dance and fit right in with the crowd. My mother and father make great dancing partners and seem to relish reliving their graduation and celebrating their engagement that took place that same day.

My acceptance at Farleigh College of Music is still a sore subject at home. However, this night Dad makes a startling admission. "Grady, classical music can sometimes be dry and monotonous, whereas contemporary music makes participants out of spectators."

I'm moved to tears. I realize how much it took for Dad to say that, especially since I bucked him regarding Juilliard. Wonder if dancing with Mom to my music was instrumental in the sudden change of heart? "Does that mean you approve of my enrolling at Farleigh?"

"You'd make your mark wherever you went, son," Dad says and pats me on the back. "I'd be disappointed if you didn't far surpass all the Winslows."

ASHLEY

It's 1983 and I'm the valedictorian of my graduating class at Central.

"Ashley, you look lovely," Mom says as she fusses with my hair. We had spent almost the entire day looking for a knock-out dress.

Dad complains, "That's an awfully expensive dress just to be hidden by her graduation gown."

"This is a once-in-a-lifetime event," Mom says and frowns at Dad. Dad very wisely aborts his criticism.

At the graduation ceremony, I'm so nervous my stomach churns and my hands shake when I sing the National Anthem as a prelude to commencement. Though I have been a regular feature at all our sporting events for the past two years, this day is different. I gaze out into the crowd and spot my parents and both sets of grandparents. They stand a little more erect than most of the others. I'm not sure whether they're proud or just as nervous as me. Relief replaces apprehension when I hear the roar of the crowd as I conclude.

ASHLEY

My father did not seem to be as upset as I thought he'd be when I applied for and was accepted at Farleigh College of Music in Boston. "We hate to see you go so far from home," he said, "but you'll be near and dear to your mother and me wherever you go."

"Good choice of careers," Mom says. "I'll never forget what your Great Aunt Lucinda told me the day I left for college, "Embark on a career you love and embrace it with all your might. After all, it's not what you do but how you do it."

CHAPTER TWO

Right Frame of Mind

GRADY

I've been bunking with Charlie and Freddie and it's now the start of my third year at Farleigh College of Music. The three of us have lived in the same apartment complex since arriving in Boston. Unlike Juilliard, first year students are not required to live in student housing. We divided up the domestic chores when we moved in together, and since Charlie likes to cook, Freddie and I do the dishes and house cleaning. Charlie likes to explore his surroundings and is a man about campus. In contrast, Freddie and I are pretty much home bodies.

Although The New York Five has gigs here and there, we have not found our niche. Our jam sessions are fun but we've been told by several of those in the know that we are destined for failure unless we find a classy female vocalist.

• • •

The first week of the semester, on my way to class, I pass by one of the cubicles reserved for practice. I pause when I hear the beat of background music and the sultry voice of a female singing our band's theme song, *Right Frame of Mind*. Peering through the small window in the door, I stand and listen to the all too familiar lyrics:

> You can:
> Travel to planet Mars
> Or go dance with the stars
> Find happiness in small things
> Everything's not as it seems
> When you're in the right frame of mind

You can:
Make good use of your time
Change your life on a dime
Count your blessings and be glad
Smile, be happy, throw off sad
When you're in the right frame of mind.

You can:
Take my hand, follow me
And find a brand new day
Love's a gift like rain and sun
It's free, it's for everyone
When you're in the right frame of mind

Will you:
Open your heart, let me in
Nothing to lose, only win
When you say that you'll be mine
I'll treasure you for all time
And we'll keep that right frame of mind

I'm mesmerized not just by the voice but by the source of the voice. As I stand transfixed, the music stops and an angelic face framed in blond hair turns toward me. In seconds my eyes are impaled in turquoise eyes as piercing as any I've ever encountered. Her quizzical gleam softens and I'm drawn into a sparkle that conveys a hidden promise. I've never believed in the adage *love at first sight,* that is until now.

"Have I exceeded the time limit?" she asks looking at her watch as she swings open the door.

I fumble around trying to think of something brilliant to say. "Ah…no," is all I finally manage, still captivated by the loveliness of this creature.

Placing her hands on her hips and looking me square in the eye, she asks in a saucy voice, "Who are you?"

I point to the piano, "I'm the composer of the song you just sang and it's our band's theme song. My name is Grady Winslow. And by the way, who's asking?"

Judging by the shocked look on her face, I must have come across like an ogre because she stammers, "I'm Ashley, Ashley Harden. I'm a freshman." She's still stammering when she says, "I found the music in a stack in the piano bench. I liked the lyrics and… I hope it was okay for me to…"

"Yes, in fact, it was more than okay—especially since you stated you liked it." I regret causing her anxiety, so hoping to reassure her, I extend my hand and say, "I'm a junior here at Farleigh and am happy to meet you. Just call me Grady, everyone does."

I tingle when she takes my hand with both of hers and says, "I'm pleased to meet you, Grady Winslow." Then looking thoughtful, she says, "You say it's your theme song and you wrote it. Do you perform?"

My heart is pounding like a bass drum and I'm hoping my nerves don't betray me. I rein in my emotions and answer, "Have you heard of The New York Five?" I'm disappointed when Ashley shakes her head.

ASHLEY

Wow, he's an upperclassman and a handsome one at that.

My hands, I suspect, are clammy and I instinctively wipe them off on the sides of my jeans. When I see the perplexed look on Grady's face, I hasten to cover by adding, "Sorry, my hands are sticky. I hope I didn't get any of my soda on you."

Grady smiles. "Wouldn't matter if you did." Then I watch as he gestures down the corridor and says, "I was just heading down to get a cold drink of my own, a soda or some iced tea. Care to join me?"

I blush. "Thank you, yes I would." I retrieve my CD and the

empty soda can and move toward the door.

"You forgot your purse." Grady points toward my purse lying on the table.

I blush again. "Do you always have this effect on women?"

"What do you mean?" Grady smiles, giving me a quizzical look.

"I'm not accustomed to being disorganized." I instantly like his boyish mannerisms and I suspect he knows exactly what I meant.

As we walk down the hall, my roommate, Carla Marston, calls to me, "You weren't going to leave without me, were you?"

I stop and put my hand to my forehead. I'm beyond embarrassed. This certainly isn't like me. First I leave my purse behind and now I start to leave without Carla. I take Grady's arm and pull him to a halt and we turn and wait for Carla. When she catches up, I introduce them. "Carla is my roommate," I say to Grady. And to Carla, I say "This is Grady Winslow. He's an upperclassman." The two shake hands.

"Ashley, I thought you didn't know anybody here," Carla says sarcastically, as she sizes up Grady.

"Didn't until about two minutes ago." Then I hook my arm through his. "I hope I get to know him better."

Now Grady blushes. "I hope you do, too," he finally manages.

Whatta ya know, this upperclassman is just as mesmerized with me as I am with him.

We go to the kiosk in the student union building and Carla joins us for iced tea. Carla and I sit transfixed as Grady educates us on Farleigh, its benefits and detriments. After an hour, Carla excuses herself. Grady and I watch her leave, and after she's gone, I look at my watch. "I need to go, too."

Grady says, "Can I have your phone number?"

"Only if I can have yours," I reply.

I'm still on cloud nine when I arrive back at our bachelor pad. I flop down on the futon, put my legs up and casually announce to Charlie and Freddie that I have discovered the quintessential lead female vocalist for our band and the quintessential leading lady of my life.

"That wouldn't be Ashley Harden, would it?" Charlie asks, without looking up from the book he'd been studying.

I immediately sit up, staring at Charlie, "How in the hell?"

Closing the book, Charlie returns my stare and replies, "She's the one I took to the movies Monday night."

"The one you said was as hot as a firecracker?"

"One and the same!"

In an instant my world crumbles around me. I can't believe my ears and am perplexed when I come to the realization that I must not be the only one.

• • •

The following Friday, whether out of pride or disappointment, I don't call Ashley. Instead, I go bowling with Nadine Brockland, a girl I have been dating off and on since my freshman year here at Farleigh. Although I'm with Nadine, my mind is on Ashley.

"You seem to be distracted," Nadine says and I detect disappointment in her voice.

"What? Oh, sorry, Nadine. I, ah, I've been working on a composition and my mind keeps reverting back to my creation. Would you prefer to go somewhere else?"

"Why don't you just take me home. I'm not having that much fun anyway and it doesn't appear you are either."

"Okay, if that's what you want."

"Sounds like that's what *you* want. You seem to have changed since our last date. We don't kid around and laugh like we used to. You've become way too serious."

"Guess this has been a bust. It was not intended to be. Again, my apologies."

"Just take me home and don't call me again."

When I leave Nadine at her dorm, I head home. I'm ashamed of the way I ignored Nadine and I hope I can make it up to her someday. *Is this the effect of being in love?* I always thought love was supposed to be a wonderful experience, but so far, not so in my case. Can't erase Ashley from my mind.

When I return home, I notice I have a message from Ashley. "Call me even if it's late." I'm still wallowing in embarrassment, mostly because of my preoccupation with Ashley, and after my conversation with Charlie, I'm not sure I want to call her back. That thought, however, doesn't linger. The next thing I know, I'm dialing Ashley's number.

"This is Ashley."

The sound of her voice gives me goosebumps. "Ashley, Grady here. Just picked up your message."

I notice she sounds like she's out of breath when she says, "I wasn't sure if you were to call me or I was to call you."

"Don't think we discussed that. Anyway, I'm glad you called," I say, and because of her breathlessness, I ask, "Is this a bad time?"

"No, not at all. I was on the balcony and had to run to catch the phone, I was hoping it was you," she says, explaining the breathlessness. "Tomorrow's Saturday and I thought we might get together and commandeer a studio with a piano."

"Swell, the band is thinking of adding a vocalist. Want to try out?"

"I'd like that. You can play and I'll audition."

"You're on!"

"Afterwards, we can have lunch at Cal's Grill on Copley Square—my treat."

"I can do that...but only if I buy. Deal?"

"Only if I can buy the next time. Deal?"

"How can I refuse."

...

Ashley's voice and my accompaniment mesh like bees and honey. Honey describes Ashley's voice. It's sweet and melodious. I don't know whether it's Ashley or her voice that enamors me. Before the jam session ends, I'm falling madly and hopelessly in love. What about Charlie's revelation? I know Charlie is prone to exaggeration—especially when it comes to his supposed conquests. Besides, Ashley hadn't met me yet and couldn't have made an informed decision if indeed what Charlie intimated was true. *What dumb luck! I must be living right. A beautiful woman and a beautiful voice all rolled up in one!*

For the first time without so much as a rehearsal, we both agree the performance is spectacular. "You're fabulous on a piano and your voice sends chills down my spine," Ashley says.

"Both the voice and the woman are beautiful. No wonder you have all the men on campus swooning, including my roommate."

"Who's your roommate?" Ashley asks, squinting as though she didn't know.

"Charles Morgan." I watch for her reaction.

"Please! You've got to be kidding. I have more discerning taste than Charlie." Ashley grimaces.

"You mean he struck out?" Even I can detect the hopefulness in my voice. She must have also detected it.

She looks up at me with a provocative grin, "Things might have been different if it had been his roommate."

"You mean Freddie?"

"No, silly, you."

I flush. "You're not prone to exaggeration too, are you?"

"I find you fascinating and irresistible." Ashley raises her brow and flutters her eyelashes.

"You're the first co-ed I've met that could make Miss Universe feel insecure."

Ashley is standing on the opposite side of the piano. She crosses her arms, and leaning toward me, asks, "Are you talking about beauty, smarts or talent?"

"All three." I run my fingers the length of the keyboard to punctuate my answer.

The sparkle in her eyes and the smile on her lips tells me I'm not the only one aware of her attributes. Vanity has its own mystique, and her flare unmistakably conveys a hidden promise—the same one I had detected the day we met.

"I would like for you to join The New York Five," I say.

"Without talking to the others?" she asks.

"Yes! Even if it means just the two of us, I think we should do it."

Again, her patented twinkle and smile. "Are we talking about the band or something else?"

"It's negotiable." We both laugh. She comes around the piano to where I'm sitting and gives me a kiss full on the lips. It is hot and moist. My mind takes me in another direction, but only momentarily. My father warned me not to mix business with pleasure. Now was not the moment to flout his advice. But then again....

"You'll have to rename the group if there are six," Ashley says reflectively. Other than Charlie Morgan, who are the others?"

"Freddie McIntire, Bobby Jenkins and Denny Fleming. Charlie and Freddie are guitarists. Bobby has replaced Jimmy on the drums and Denny has replaced Danny on the sax."

Ashley looks pensive. "The New York Six somehow doesn't have the same ring as The New York Five."

"No, but Ashley and The New York Five does," I say.

From Ashley's reaction, I know I've hit a homerun over the center field fence. Being the messenger this time has its perks. I sense Ashley is developing the same feelings for me as I am for her.

• • •

With a female vocalist like Ashley, it was not long before we catapulted to the top. Soon we had bookings not only for Friday nights but Saturday nights as well at the famous Boston Dubois on

Copley Square.

By the way, after our jam session, I drove Ashley down to Cal's Grill on Copley Square and we both ordered hot pastrami on pumpernickel. We sat in a booth by a window and we engaged in frivolous conversation as we sipped the limeades and devoured the sandwiches. We compared our likes and dislikes and the more we talked the more serious and philosophical we became. She impressed me with her candid disclosures, and I found myself soon following suit. We agreed on more than we disagreed on. When it came to politics, we had the same leanings and high-fived each other when she announced she voted for the person not necessarily the party affiliation.

When I return back to the apartment, Charlie and Freddie quiz me on my first date with Ashley. They want chapter and verse. I must admit I borrowed Charlie's thunder and turn a walk in the park into a fantasyland. Both of my roommates stare in wonder as I narrate events that usually happen only in X-rated novels. I'm amazed at my imagination, and feeling guilty about the deceit, I readily admit to Charlie and Freddie it's only a spoof.

"For a minute there, I believed you," Charlie says.

Wonder what that implies?

• • •

The glamour and glitz of the Boston Dubois spurred us on to bigger and better performances. Soon we were packing them in. Watching patrons standing in line to find seating was more of a testament to Ashley than the rest of us. She was a natural and "wowed them" as the manager of the Boston Dubois was heard to say.

Despite Ashley's popularity and desirability, she remained loyal to the group, and amazingly enough, to me. When our performances began competing with our education, we were forced to make choices and set priorities. All, except Charlie, were in favor of limiting our performances when they conflicted timewise or otherwise with school or school-related activities.

The lure of fame and fortune was tempting. However, we felt that in the long run we had little choice but to tough out the competing allegiances to school—which we did. All of us were involved in one or more of the musicals at Farleigh and Ashley and I had the leads in one of my all-time favorites, *South Pacific*.

During our final performance of *South Pacific*, I met Ashley's parents, Dr. Timothy Harden and Roslyn Harden. Ashley's mother was an older version of Ashley not only in looks but personality as well. It was obvious the Hardens had a swimming pool or access to one and that Roslyn was a sun worshiper. That Dr. Harden was a doting husband was evident from the diamond rings his wife sported on the fourth finger of each hand. The one on the right hand was almost the size of the Hope Diamond. Considering what the medical profession charges by the hour, it should have been the size of an ice cube.

CHAPTER THREE

_____

Don't Give Me Tomorrow

GRADY

By the time Ashley had completed her second year at Farleigh, she had taken Basic Keyboard 1 and 2, Advanced Counterpoint and Techniques of Tonal Writing. In addition to the above, I had completed courses in Style Analysis; Instrumental and Score Preparation; Contemporary Techniques in Composition 1 and 2; Scoring for Full Orchestra; and Directed Study in Sonata and Orchestral Composition.

Between the two of us, we had all the bases covered and collaborated on our first musical composition together which we titled ***Don't Give Me Tomorrow.*** Compared to our later compositions, it paled. However, at the time we were ecstatic, and Ashley sang it like it was the most romantic song ever written. Just using our own composition and sheet music with our names listed as composers was a high. The following are the lyrics to that song:

> Don't give me tomorrow
> I need you right now
> Don't add to my sorrow
> I want to be your lover, baby
> Won't you tell me how?
>
> I don't need a promise
> I don't need a vow
> Life is just a gamble
> Won't you take me now?

Don't give me tomorrow
Take me day by day
Let me share your sorrows
Let me help you find your way

Through each rainy day
Help you find your way
Help you find your way
Today may be that day

CHAPTER FOUR

Ashley

GRADY

As I reflect on my time with Ashley, my imagination kicks into overdrive. If only someone like that could love me… It is not long before I begin to formulate a song to coincide with my unbridled feelings, and considering I've never been in love before, I'm surprised the lyrics come so easily. It's entitled *Ashley*.

> Ashley, Ashley, you are always on my mind
> You mean more all the time
> How can I ever be
> The same without you?
>
> Ashley, Ashley, you came into my life
> You brought me much delight
> To be loved by you
> I will always love you too
>
> *You brighten up my life*
> *I can't believe it's true*
> *To be loved by you*
> *I will always love you too*
>
> Ashley, Ashley, you are my dream come true
> I feel your love come through
> How can I ever be
> The same without you?
>
> Ashley, Ashley, you're in my mind and heart
> We'll never be apart

A miracle came to me
I'll never feel this way again

You brighten up my life
I can't believe it's true
To be loved by you
I will always love you too

Ashley, Ashley, you're my ray of hope
The bright spot in my day
How can I ever be
The same without you?

Ashley, Ashley, you'll never be alone
I'll always be here for you
For here's where I belong
Where I can sing your song

You brighten up my life
I can't believe it's true
To be loved by you
I will always love you too

CHAPTER FIVE

Can't Live Without You

GRADY

College life was a whirlwind experience. At the time I felt I was on a roller coaster. There never was a day I second-guessed going to Farleigh. Even Dad had grown accustomed to my selection of an avocation that some might consider frivolous. Then again, he had done the same thing.

I spent summers at home assisting Dad in family enterprises during the week. On the weekends, The New York Five was on display living a musical dream. Ashley wasn't part of the summer group until the summer after my senior year at Farleigh. That would have been the summer between her sophomore and junior years. At the time, she was living in the guest quarters of our home. That portion of what the town folks refer to as Winslow Mansion consisted of a drawing/study room, over-sized bedroom, vanity and bathroom, double-size closet, and a balcony overlooking our swimming pool. As if it were built with Ashley in mind, she had access to the music room on the ground floor through a spiral staircase that led from the drawing/study room. The music room was large enough to accommodate the two baby grand pianos on which Dad and I played classical duets.

It was probably living together in the same household that made our relationship really begin to blossom. Though my parents were present most of the time and her parents, when in New York, stayed with us, we had our intimate moments. We were described by family and friends as being inseparable. That was an apt description. I was convinced early on that I could not live without Ashley and hoped she felt the same about me.

. . .

Although living a dream, I wasn't oblivious to reality. Early in our relationship, I began to have suspicions about Ashley's fidelity. The first was Charlie's description of his encounter with her. Since that episode, if indeed it happened, occurred before we had even started dating, I wrote it off as inconsequential. However, the seed was planted, and I was more vigilant than I probably would have been otherwise.

Shortly after Ashley joined The New York Five, Charlie's cousin, Darrius Ayres, a stockbroker from Chicago, arrived in town. He had a football player's build, dark curly hair and a glow that suggested he spent a lot of time either on the tennis court or the golf course. As it turned out, his hobbies included both. However, the time he spent on his yacht was unquestionably responsible for what he bragged was a full body copper tan.

It was September and Darrius was staying at the Crayton Plaza, a hotel known for its clientele. Reputedly, the Kennedys and other celebrities and notables stayed there. Darrius had a penthouse suite. He and his business associate were hosting a cocktail party following a broker's conference. Charlie had volunteered our band to provide the entertainment.

The guests included a number of women who did not fit the broker profile. I asked Charlie if they were the wives of the brokers. He just laughed and said, "The portfolios they put together contain stock that is not traded on the traditional stock exchanges. You might say they are private offerings."

"I take it Darrius didn't bring his wife with him."

"Although Stephanie is a trophy, you seldom see them together."

I glance around the room. "He seems to be spending a lot of time with the Farrah Fawcett lookalike."

Charlie looks at the pair standing by the wet bar and says, "That's his assistant, Laurissa Flegmon. She's his right-hand gal!"

"They must work closely together. Right now he can't keep his hands off her," I comment.

"Yep, noticed that myself," Charlie says with a wry smile. Then he adds, "Can you blame him?"

I don't bother answering his rhetorical question.

During the break, I notice Darrius strike up a conversation with Ashley. I'm on high alert because of my suspicions regarding Ashley and red flags are raised when Darrius continues to hold onto Ashley's hand. I experience some jealously and have to admit that if Darrius is the competition, I don't have a chance. When I turn to speak to Charlie, Darrius and Ashley disappear. I do a sweeping inspection of the room and don't see either one of them. I'm seeped in anxiety and attempt to disguise my emotions as I sit at the keyboard thumbing through sheet music. Feeling like a lovesick schoolboy, I try to suppress what I'm thinking. My instincts tell me what's happening, but I try not to give in to those thoughts. The rumors I've heard around campus that Ashley is a *yes girl*, and my own observations, reinforced by Charlie's comments, cause me a great deal of misery. I'm apprehensive about Ashley disappearing with Darrius and find it hard to concentrate on the performance.

It appears as though the guests are getting restless, so when Ashley doesn't return, Charlie suggests we begin without her. I fear I won't be able to control my anger and frustration so I just nod. We go through a couple of numbers and when Ashley finally rejoins us, her hair is disheveled, and her face is flushed. She doesn't look at me when she approaches. Although I try to draw her attention by standing and beckoning to her with my hands, she does not respond. I'm tempted to ask her where the hell she's been but am hesitant to do so. This is not the time or place to start a quarrel over Ashley's infidelity. The Five deserve better. The next number is a duet and as I move from the keyboard to the mic, Ashley flashes me a smile as if nothing is amiss. I guess in her world, all's fair in love and war.

After our last number, I pull Ashley aside and ask her, "It's not like you to miss or be late for a number. What happened?" I watch that here we go again expression cross her face. If she expects me to back down, she's mistaken. I cross my arms and stand my ground waiting for an answer.

"I was waylaid," was her only explanation. When I attempt to pursue the point, we're interrupted by Charlie. "Darrius wants us to join his table—all six of us," he says. *Of course he does!* My anger resurfaces and I'm tempted to walk away. However, in the midst of my indecision, Ashley grabs me by the arm and says, "Oh, come on, Grady. He's old enough to be my daddy. There's room in my heart for only one love." She kisses me on the cheek and drags me to Darrius' table.

When we arrive at the table, Laurissa is seated to Darrius' right. He looks up at Ashley with what appears to be lust in his eyes and motions for her to sit in the empty chair to his left. I notice Laurissa shoot him a disapproving glance. She's probably in the same boat as I am. Ashley loops her arm through mine and snuggles close to me. She shakes her head at Darrius and signals with her hand that she will sit beside me. That gesture convinces me that I've probably made an unwarranted assumption. Ashley positions her chair closer to mine and treats me as though I'm the only man in the room. To me, however, the elephant is still Darrius.

Later, on the way home, when I bring up Darrius' name, Ashley says, "Grady, must we? He's a total bore. Let's talk about his generous tip. A five grand night is nothing to sneeze at!"

That was almost double what our gigs usually brought in. Wonder what else the tip included. However, I let the matter drop. I've come to realize this is Ashley's *modus operandi.* She heaps it on me, pushing me away, and when she realizes she's gone too far and she may really be losing me, she pulls me back in with some ingratiating gesture. And fool that I am, I go on as if nothing happened. But each of Ashley's indiscretions exacts a toll and I feel our relationship is eroding bit by bit. It bothered me then and bothers me now.

• • •

I'm still obsessing over an incident that occurred when Ashley was a junior and I was getting my master's degree at Farleigh and taking several classical music courses. The latter was at the encouragement of my father who still wanted me to be a concert pianist.

As Christmas break approached, Ashley told me she wanted to spend Christmas in Colorado with her family. I opted to spend Christmas in New York with my parents since Ashley would be gone over the holidays. Ashley's traveling companions were two boys from Farleigh and one of Ashley's roommates, Corrine Caldwell, who was also from Grand Junction. At the time, I thought nothing of it.

Soon after Ashley returned to Farleigh after Christmas break, she announced that her long-time roommate, Carla Marsten, who Ashley introduced me to the day we met, was moving out. Ashley and I had double dated on numerous occasions with Carla and her boyfriend, Rob Harris. When I questioned Ashley about Carla's unanticipated departure, she said she didn't want to talk about it. Needless to say, this bit of news came as a surprise since Ashley had been gone for two weeks. *What could have possibly happened to cause a rift in the short time Ashley has been back?* Ashley's attitude was disturbing, and I was perplexed because I thought Ashley and Carla were best friends.

Several days after this revelation, I run into Carla at the FCM bookstore. When she spots me, she immediately turns and walks in the other direction. What the hell's going on? I hurry to catch up to her.

"Carla, it's me, Grady," I call out as I quicken my pace. As I draw near, she turns and faces me. I notice tears well up in her eyes.

"I don't want to talk to you." She stops in her tracks and pulls a tissue from her pocket and dabs at her eyes.

When I try to comfort her, she breaks down completely.

"What?" I ask.

"It's not you, it's Ashley!" she sobs.

"Did something happen?" I was afraid of what the answer might be. Carla nods, and as I glance around, I notice other students are staring at us. Carla's sobs were now interlaced with hiccups, so I lead her outside to a stone bench where I try to console her.

"It's okay," I say, as I hand her my handkerchief.

"It's not okay!" Carla blurts. She swipes at the cascade of tears streaming down her cheeks. "Ashley and Rob..."

"Ashley and Rob what?" I brace myself for the answer. I know what's coming. Carla just shakes her head, apparently unable to get control of her emotions. I take her hand, hoping my gesture will spur her on to continue. Although I'm anxious to know what happened, I'm reluctant to face the inevitable.

After Carla calms down, she asks, "Did you know that one of the students that Ashley rode home with was Rob?"

"No, all I knew was that she was traveling home with three other students from Colorado." I pause and rub my brow. A sick feeling engulfs me and my heart sinks. "Did something happen between Ashley and Rob?"

"Yes! The two of them made out in the back seat."

There it was, right in my face. When I close my eyes, Carla grabs me by the arm. "I didn't want to tell you."

With my eyes still closed, I just shake my head. After what seems like an eternity, I ask, "How'd you know?"

"The driver was Lloyd Young, a close friend of mine. In fact, he and I dated when I first came to Farleigh." Carla twists my handkerchief in her hands and looks away. Then looking back at me, she says, "Lloyd told me."

I feel like crying myself. "Did you confront Rob?"

Carla looks away again for a brief moment. "It took some doing, but I pulled it out of him." Carla laughs without humor, "Rob swore it was nothing. However, Rob's version doesn't support Lloyd's, and I'm inclined to believe Lloyd."

I nod. I'm sickened not only for myself but for Carla. Ashley passed Carla off as her best friend in addition to being her roommate. Where I come from, you don't treat friends like that. "Where are you living now?" I ask.

Carla shrugs. "I moved in with Irene and Katrina."

"Did you and Ashley have a heated argument?"

"Not really. However, I could have scratched her eyes out. The fact is I was more upset by the way Ashley acted when I confronted her than by what she and Rob did behind my back. We weren't just roommates, we were best friends."

I again nod. "That's Ashley."

Carla sniffles and dabs at her nose. "You deserve better. The betrayal cost me my boyfriend, my best friend and my trust in my fellow classmates. Not sure which I miss the most."

• • •

Later, I confront Ashley.

"Sounds like you don't trust me," she says, without making eye contact.

Well, here we go again, turning things around and putting me on the defensive. "All I want is the truth," I say.

"You wouldn't believe me if I told you, it was much ado about nothing," Ashley says as she examines her nails.

"Making out in the backseat with Rob was nothing?" I blurt. "Not only did you betray my trust, but the two of you all but destroyed Carla."

"Oh, please! That rumor is just wishful thinking on Rob's part," she says and walks away. In true Ashley fashion, she attempts to dismiss the incident as rumor perpetrated by Rob, attempting to put the blame on him.

When I arrive back at my apartment, I have a message on my answering machine. It is from Ashley. "Grady, I want to apologize for leaving so abruptly. Why would I ever do anything that would jeopardize our relationship? Nothing is worth losing you. I'll give you space to think about it. If you still feel the same after a few days and want to call it quits, I'll understand. Otherwise, I'll be here for you." *More pushing me away and pulling me back. She's driving me crazy but I find life without her is dismal at best.*

For the next several days, Ashley and I avoid each other. More aptly, it's me who avoids her. It's difficult not to relent and contact Ashley. Whenever I retrieve my telephone messages, I'm disappointed there are no other messages from Ashley. Still, I'm determined not to make the next move. It hurts but I feel I have no choice.

On the afternoon of the third day without Ashley, I go to *our* cubicle at Farleigh and compose a song I entitle **Can't Live Without You**. The lyrics go something like this:

> Every time I look at you
> I know exactly what to do
> Come here close and look into my eyes
> You're the only one I idolize
>
> Take my hand and hold it tight
> The things we do seem oh so right
> You're the only one I want to know
> Pull me close and never let me go
>
> *I need you every minute*
> *Of every hour of every day*
> *I can't live without you*
> *Seems there is no other way*
> *I need you every minute*
> *Of every hour of every day*
> *Oh, I can't live without you*
> *There is no other way*
>
> Time stands still when I'm with you
> When you're gone I am so blue
> Reach for me and take me in your arms
> You're the only one with such charms

I want to spend my life with you
No one else would ever do
I'll hold you near for all eternity
Won't you come and share your life with me

I need you every minute
Of every hour of every day
I can't live without you
Seems there is no other way
I need you every minute
Of every hour of every day
Oh, I can't live without you
There is no other way

My heart dictates the lyrics as well as the melody. It flows sweet and true. I'm so caught up in the moment and my attention drawn to the piano that I'm unaware that I'm not alone. It is only when I finish my rendition and hear loud applause behind me that I realize someone else has entered the cubicle that had once been Ashley's and my little musical hideaway.

"That was beautiful!" Tears stream down her cheeks. "Did you write that for me?"

Ashley's presence startles me. Relief washes over me as I realize that I really can't live without her and that no one else would ever do.

"Life without you would never be the same." I stand and she rushes into my arms.

CHAPTER SIX

Not the Only One

GRADY

Charlie had been my best friend through grade school, high school, and four years at Farleigh. I was hesitant to discuss my relationship with Ashley with him because of his hint of intimacy with her prior to she and I having met. Since I had no one else to share my concerns with, I confided in Charlie one morning as we cleared the breakfast clutter from the tiny nook in our apartment.

"Charlie, taming Ashley would be like trying to tame a wildcat. The odds are I can't."

"I've been trying to tell you that for over two years," Charlie said as he placed the orange juice back in the refrigerator. Then he turned to me. "Something else happen?"

When I told Charlie about the latest in a series of episodes, he just shook his head.

"Well?" I coaxed.

Charlie raised his brow. "Do you really want me to level with you?"

"I respect your judgment."

"You're not going to like my slant."

"Try me."

"You have been blinded by the charms of a she-devil and by playing with fire, you're eventually going to get burned." Charlie tossed the tea towel he'd been using to dry the dishes over his shoulder and looked me straight in the eye. "She's already scorched your feathers. But you seem hell bent on making a fool out of yourself and there's nothing I can do to get you to throw in the towel." He slammed the tea towel onto the counter.

I got the message, but still looking for a solution, I pled my case. "You don't understand. Ashley's the first woman I've met that confirms there's such a thing as true love."

"Keep on dreaming, Grady. It sounds to me like the true love is a one-way street. Odds are that you'll get jilted or wish you had."

• • •

Bobby Jenkins, our drummer, decided to move on to bigger and better things, so when he left the band, he was replaced by Tommy Del Rio. Tommy had been a drummer for a number of well-known bands and performed in several of the lounges in Las Vegas. His reputation tagged him as a drifter, and he had difficulty finding permanent work. We were unable to find a drummer of his caliber, so we decided to take a chance and settled for Tommy. Of Latin descent, he sported a tan that was not fed by the sun. Though he was in his twenties, he could easily pass for much older, as his lifestyle was taking its toll. He'd been in and out of rehab, and we knew we had a problem on our hands.

Ashley had been Tommy's target from the first day. I, for one, did not think he was a threat, as his only contact with Ashley was during practices and performances when we were all together.

The band was thriving as never before, and it was evident that Tommy was a welcome addition and his solos a hit with the younger set. With Tommy's track record, he surprised us when he missed very few practices.

One hot July afternoon we were scheduled to practice our numbers for a gig at the Fourth of July celebration at the Boston Cosmopolitan Hotel. We had added several new numbers to our repertoire and were eager to get started. When Ashley and Tommy had not appeared at the appointed hour, that raised red flags all over the place.

I looked at Charlie and he just raised his brow and shrugged his shoulders when I asked if we should go ahead and get started. With

Ashley's track record, I was suspicious and even angry. After playing a series of songs, Ashley finally showed up, followed minutes later by Tommy.

"Sorry I'm late," she said. "Got tied up in a construction zone." Tommy's excuse was that he had a flat tire.

Over the next several weeks Ashley would disappear for larger and larger blocks of time. Her feeble excuses did not appease me. When she joined a health club, she became even scarcer. Although I tried to follow her from time to time, I would lose her in heavy traffic or crowds.

I suppose it was obvious even to Ashley that I was fed up with her antics. I assumed that she had tuned into my moods. When I became distant, Ashley would pull me back in with her sweet talk. I had become more resilient, and Ashley and I seemed to be growing apart. By August, we saw each other infrequently. With the start of my second year in graduate school and Ashley's senior year, I had made several trips to New York to see my parents; Ashley made roughly the same number of trips to be with her parents in Grand Junction.

After one of my trips home, I arrived back in Boston a day earlier than expected and attempted to reach her by phone. I had reflected on my relationship with Ashley and had come to the conclusion that I was just being paranoid. I rationalized that, after all, Ashley was a sought-after commodity, a one of a kind. Why wouldn't a guy be attracted to her? Although there was an unspoken commitment of fidelity between us, there was no binding covenant such as an engagement. Though I was considering such an overture, something in the back of my mind told me to wait. With her propensity toward the opposite sex, I wasn't sure even an engagement ring would rein her in. However, one thing I was sure of was that I could no longer turn a blind eye to her infidelity.

It was nearing ten p.m. and when I dialed Ashley's number and received the same message, all kinds of thoughts raced through my mind. Foremost was the vivid image of Ashley seated with the silhouette of a man having drinks at a tavern resembling that of the Blue Haven Lounge at the Boston Cosmopolitan Hotel.

Common sense said let it be. *But when did I ever use common sense when it came to Ashley?* Being compulsive, I drove to the Boston Cosmopolitan Hotel, almost daring the fuzz to stop me. After parking in a loading zone and dashing into the hotel lobby, I began having second thoughts. *Do I want to do this? What if I find Ashley with another man? What do I do then?* I considered retreating. Something kept urging me on and I knew if I didn't find out, it would haunt me forever. I took a deep breath and marched into the dimly lit lounge amid the din of laughter and frivolous conversation.

I caught sight of Ashley in the pose I had imagined, dressed to the hilt and engrossed in conversation with a man I did not recognize. The two were seated opposite each other at a small table with drinks in front of them. Their hands were entwined and their eyes on each other.

Impulsively, I went up to the table, and spurred by anger, hurt, and disappointment, I said to Ashley, "What the hell are you doing here?" She jerked around at the sound of my voice and her eyes widened and her jaw dropped. If she said anything, I didn't hear it. I clenched my fists and abruptly turned and disappeared into the night without saying another word. Even now, everything is a blur.

I cancelled our band's next scheduled practice and spent the afternoon at the piano. My heart ached as I composed the song I later dubbed *Not The Only One.*

> I remember the day you entered my life
> I saw the light
> The room was all aglow
> You told me I was the center of your universe
> The shining star
> The only one you ever wanted to know

I know I'm not the only one
Not the only one who shares their love with you
I know I'm not the only one
Not the only one who wakes up next to you
I know you have a lot to give
A lot to give
A lot you want to share
I know you have a lot of love
A lot of love
But not enough to go around

I remember you standing there beside me
I needed you
You were my heart and soul
You told me you could not live without me
Life would never be the same
I was the only one you ever loved

I know I'm not the only one
Not the only one who shares their love with you
I know I'm not the only one
Not the only one who wakes up next to you
I know you have a lot to give
A lot to give
A lot you want to share
I know you have a lot of love
A lot of love
But not enough to go around

I can't forget the day
I saw you with someone new
Seated next to you
You broke my heart in two
No one told me I couldn't live without you
Life could never be the same

I wasn't the only one you ever loved

I know I'm not the only one
Not the only one who shares their love with you
I know I'm not the only one
Not the only one who wakes up next to you
I know you have a lot to give
A lot to give
A lot you want to share
I know you have a lot of love
A lot of love
But not enough to go around

Maybe I'm wise or maybe I'm foolish
Maybe I shouldn't stay away
But you know I can't stand in line
Waiting to see if you're really mine
Oh, you can't be the only one
No, you can't be the only one around

The third verse still brings tears to my eyes. Seeing Ashley with someone new was like living a bad dream. It was a crushing blow.

CHAPTER SEVEN

It's You Who I See

GRADY

I tried to write Ashley off as a lost cause. No matter how hard I tried, Ashley continued to haunt me, and I couldn't get her out of my mind. I thought about her every waking hour and dreamt about her when I fell asleep. Even after we replaced Ashley and changed the name of our band, I still felt lost.

Dorinda Denton was a sophomore music student at Farleigh. Dorinda had the looks and presence of someone you would expect to see on a movie screen. She had a voice to match. The switch from Ashley to Dorinda was an easy one and soon our band was known as Dorinda and The New York Five.

Ashley had described Dorinda as conceited and aloof. I knew from the start that Ashley disliked Dorinda mainly out of jealousy and considered her competition. The previous summer, at a barbeque at Ashley's apartment complex, Dorinda, who also lived in the complex, was present. Some of the residents were engaging in a game of water volleyball in the complex swimming pool. I was urged to join in. Dorinda and I ended up on the same team. None of the players were very good and we had a blast laughing and making fun of each other. At the end of the game, we were drained so I lent Dorinda a hand helping her out of the pool.

Afterwards, Ashley chastised me for flirting with Dorinda. "It's obvious Dorinda has the hots for you. You made a fool of yourself by falling all over her."

If it weren't so sad, it would be laughable. Ashley had the nerve to chastise me for interacting with another woman. Although I have never considered myself vindictive, I conceived of a plan—one, I'm ashamed to say, to this day still pangs my heart. I knew Ashley usually returned from the library around nine in the evening, so I made arrangements to take Dorinda to dinner after one of our rehearsals and then drive her to the apartment complex where she and Ashley lived.

"What is it, Grady? You keep looking at your watch." Dorinda said and pulled away.

I didn't answer. To enter the apartment complex, all residents and guests were required to pass through an atrium connected by a main office and lounge. The office contained mailboxes for the residents and was monitored by a uniformed guard after six p.m. The lounge had a fireplace and various vending machines. Being situated in close proximity to Farleigh, most of the residents were single students, mainly female. Because of strict security, many of the female students bid their dates goodbye at the door with a parting kiss, much like at a sorority house.

I knew Ashley's study habits and that she left the library, where she did her research, writing and homework, at approximately nine p.m. The scheme I hatched was to take Dorinda home a little before nine p.m. and be in the lounge facing the door with Dorinda in my arms just as Ashley entered the apartment complex.

Dorinda and I arrived at the complex just as I had planned. We went into the lounge, and as we stood by the fireplace, I kept my eyes glued on the window in the door waiting for Ashley to approach. When I saw her, I gathered Dorinda in my arms. Then, choosing my moment carefully, I kissed Dorinda goodnight. I made it appear as something more than just a casual goodnight kiss.

I watched as Ashley stopped in her tracks. I'll never forget the hurt look in her eyes and the quiver of her lips as a stream of tears flowed down her cheeks. Instead of exuberance on my part, I felt an emptiness and remorse that has, to this day, never been equaled. I used Dorinda as a ploy to even the score with Ashley and to cause unspeakable grief to the only woman I really loved. And I used an innocent third party to exact my pound of flesh. It is something I will always regret.

• • •

When I got home after dropping Dorinda off, I was told by the manager that earlier that day a dozen roses had been delivered to my apartment and were outside my door. When I got to my apartment, I retrieved a bouquet of long-stemmed roses of varying colors. Attached to the stem of one was a card that read:

> **Grady, the black roses represent my mourning us being apart, the white my desire to wipe the record clean and the red my love. Forgive my indiscretions.**
>
> **Ashley**

My own act of indiscretion in trying to even the score was at the very least insensitive. It's doubtful Ashley would have penned what she did after witnessing my encounter with Dorinda. I may still have received the roses but with a card that very well could have read:

> **Grady, the thorns remind me of you—vexing, troubling and irritating. Go to hell.**
>
> **Ashley**

• • •

Pining for Ashley occupied the better part of my waking moments the next several days. She seemed to be avoiding me like the plague, as I did not see her in the usual locations on campus. I learned the hard way that vindication exacts its own price. I was even more miserable than before. Ironically enough, the words to Elvis' last number one hit, *Suspicious Minds,* kept resurfacing, "We're caught in a trap. I can't walk out because I love you too much, baby." I feel like I'm caught in that proverbial trap, damned if I do and damned if I don't. Still, I could not bring myself to make the first overture.

I ached for Ashley. Though Dorinda didn't say anything, I sensed she was perplexed by my deceitfulness. I chose to pretty much ignore both Ashley and Dorinda. Band practices were tedious, to say the least. I had to admire Dorinda's professionalism. Even though she became as cold as ice toward me, she performed like a real trooper.

After one strenuous practice session, Charlie approached me, looking as though his patience had run its course. He pulled me aside. "What's up, Bro? The tension around here is so thick, you can cut it with a knife."

I broke down and confessed to Charlie my ill-advised indiscretion with Dorinda. I was stunned when, instead of sympathizing with me, he threw his hands up and angrily exclaimed, "Couldn't you have used someone besides our lead singer? Geeze, Grady, you gotta get a grip or we're all gonna crash and burn. Just look at those guys!" Charlie pointed to where Freddie, Denny, Tommy and Dorinda were huddled together. He then said, "Maybe you don't need a payday but the rest of us do."

I cringed. Charlie's scolding just added to my torment.

• • •

I continued to wallow in my misery. It seemed every attractive co-ed I approached on campus was Ashley until they came close enough so I could tell the difference. I even passed one with eyes as probing as Ashley's turquoise eyes. No matter where I looked, I pictured Ashley. Even when I closed my eyes, I saw Ashley.

The predicament in which I found myself dictated the writing of a song I called *It's You Who I See*. When I presented the sheet music to the band, Charlie flashed me that here-we-go- again look. After a few takes, we were ready to test our audience the following Friday. The lyrics of **It's You Who I See** was a testimonial of my state of mind and was a resounding hit.

I knew better than to walk away
Even though you begged me to stay

I saw that look in your eyes
Even then I didn't realize...that

No matter what path I take
Or what direction I go
All roads lead to you
How can it be
That no matter where I look
It's you who I see
Yes, it's you who I see

You knew that I couldn't stay away
That I would come back another day
I heard that sound in your voice
It was clear I had no choice...because

No matter what path I take
Or what direction I go
All roads lead to you
How can it be
That no matter where I look
It's you who I see
Yes, it's you who I see

You know it's difficult for me to say
That I need you each and every day
Once I felt that love in your heart
I knew we could never be apart...because

No matter what path I take
Or what direction I go
All roads lead to you
How can it be
That no matter where I look
It's you who I see
Yes, it's you who I see

Oh, I've been to many continents
Crossed many seas
Looked into many eyes
Heard many voices
And, touched many hearts
But no matter where I am or
No matter what I'm doin'
I can never be free…because
Every time I close my eyes
It's you who I see
Yes, it's you who I see

. . .

Several days after our confrontation, Charlie told me he had duplicated his copy of the sheet music to "It's You Who I See" and delivered it to Ashley. "It appears you can't live with or without her," he said as he shook his head and walked away. The next day I found an envelope addressed to me taped to our door. I recognized Ashley's unmistakable fragrance. I had trouble controlling my shaky hands as I unfolded and read the note.

> *My Dear Grady,*
> *My parents flew in from Grand Junction today. We had not seen each other since Christmas. My aunt and uncle also flew in with them. All the loves of my life are with me. All except one!*
>
> *I hope you find it in your heart to forgive me for all that I've put you through. I have been accused of pushing away anyone and everyone who shows an interest in me. I guess if someone loves me, I have this flawed feeling they must not be good enough for me. This time, my insecurity has left me stranded.*
>
> *Lasting love is not forgotten; it is merely misplaced.*
>
> *Love, Ashley*

Maybe Ashley had figured out the caper with Dorinda and had grilled Dorinda. Maybe she got the word from Tommy. Although Tommy had denied any contact with Ashley since her departure from the band, I still had my doubts. Or maybe it was the lyrics to *It's You Who I See* and her conversation with Charlie when he delivered the sheet music that spelled the difference.

It was all perplexing. On one hand, I had to admit my love for Ashley, and on the other, I harbored my misgivings about her fidelity and my inability to cope. The more I thought about it, the more I agreed with Charlie. I couldn't live with Ashley, nor could I live without her.

I was beginning to feel like a ping-pong ball going back and forth and wasn't sure on which side I belonged. One thing was sure, Ashley was accustomed to getting her way. And I was an enabler subject always to her beck and call. I put the temptation to reply to Ashley's note on hold, for the moment. I couldn't ignore her wandering ways.

When I shared Ashley's note with Charlie, he just shrugged.

"Why'd you give Ashley the sheet music to *It's You Who I See* without my permission?" I asked.

"I know you and how you feel about Ashley. You have a fixation and no matter what the odds, you'll always believe your path to happiness lies in Ashley."

• • •

When I reread Ashley's letter, I'm troubled by the last sentence. Not sure exactly what the word *misplaced* means. I want to believe it means *setting aside for the moment* and not *put in the wrong place*. I conclude I'm being much too analytical and that Ashley, in essence, is saying she's sorry and wants to make up.

Against my better judgment, I pulled out a writing pad and began jotting down my reply to her note. Not satisfied with the rough draft, I crumpled it and threw it in the trash. I repeat this several more times before penning the following:

Ashley,

The happiest moment in my life was meeting you. The lowest moment was our breakup. The most difficult is trying to erase my memory of you. The reality is I can't.

The refrain from my new song, It's You Who I See, says it all:

> *No matter what path I take*
> *Or what direction I go*
> *All roads lead to you*
> *How can it be*
> *That no matter where I look*
> *It's you who I see*
> *Yes, it's you who I see.*

I am haunted by the lyrics to that song and by your penetrating turquoise eyes. Even when I close my eyes, "It's you who I see, yes, it's you who I see."

Even though we are physically apart, you are still in my heart and will always be. Who knows? We still may be in each other's future.

Love you still,
Grady

• • •

After school the following day, I deliver my reply to Ashley's apartment complex, hoping she'll be there. After the manager promises to place the reply in Ashley's drop box, I walk over to the bay windows and gaze in the direction of the swimming pool. Ashley's absorbing the sun's rays, and I'm reminded of the lyrics to a song written by Jerome Kern and Dorothy Fields: *Lovely to look at, delightful to know and heaven to kiss.* As I linger longer than I intend, Ashley spots me and quickly wraps a beach towel around her waist and scurries in my direction.

"What are you doing here?" she asks as she slides open the door.

"Just delivered a note to you," I reply. "I gave it to the manager." As I point in the direction of the office, Ashley makes a beeline for the counter. I watch as she tears open the envelope and reads my reply. In seconds, Ashley is in my arms and her warm kiss signals surrender.

Dorinda apparently saw the handwriting on the wall and resigned from the band. Ashley is reinstated as our lead vocalist. Tommy also leaves the group. Just as well, he was a distraction. He is soon replaced by Benny Boyd, a former Farleigh classmate from Rochester. He soon proves that Tommy was not irreplaceable.

• • •

The band is in full swing, literally, as we perform at the Cosmopolitan. It is Valentine's Day 1987, Ashley's senior year and my second year of graduate school.

I'm feeling pretty good about our reconciliation, so for Valentine's Day, I buy Ashley a birthstone ring, an expensive ruby. At break, I present it to her. I have disguised it as something much larger. When she goes from several larger boxes to smaller ones and then to the velvet ring box, her eyes light up brighter than any star in the heavens.

Ashley presses the ring box close to her chest and tears fill her eyes. When I place my arms around her, she pulls me close, and I feel her soft warm lips against mine.

"Thank you," she whispers.

"But you haven't even opened it," I say.

"Don't need to," she says. And then adds, "I love you."

"I love you, too," I say. "Open it."

I'll never forget the look on Ashley's face when she opens the ring box. The look of joy rapidly turns into disappointment, her smile into a scowl.

What went wrong? I thought she'd be delighted. I'm abashed when she blurts, "It's not a diamond!" I deduce her tears are not from delight.

Attempting to be humorous and disguise my disappointment at her reaction, I reply, "But, we've only known each other for six years."

Ashley pulls away from me. Her voice cracks as she asks, "How many years does it take to fall in love?"

Since I've loved her from the moment I set my eyes on her, I don't answer. It was a rhetorical question. We sit in silence for an awkward moment; I don't know what to say. Then, after a brief pause, Ashley's expression changes and her features soften. "I'll consider this a promise ring."

I'm still shaken by Ashley's reaction when she realized the ring was not an engagement ring. "A what?" I ask.

"A promise ring, or as some refer to it, a prelude ring. A promise or prelude ring is one that precedes the real thing." Ashley gently removes the ring from the box and puts it on. She twists it around, positioning the ruby dead center on her ring finger. As she gazes at it, she says, "The ruby represents love, but unlike the diamond, does not represent true love nor a commitment to a lasting relationship."

I had done some research of my own, so I add, "The ruby is also the talisman of passion, prosperity and patience."

Ashley, looking down at the ring on her hand, says, "I'm sorry for the reaction. I'm just disappointed, that's all." She leans over and kisses me on the cheek.

CHAPTER EIGHT

You Taught Me

GRADY

One more semester and I will have my master's degree in music arrangement and orchestration. I'm uncertain as to what to do with my life. Everything is on hold depending on what Ashley does. After presenting her with the ruby ring, our relationship seems to have stabilized and I'm more inclined than ever to take that next step.

As Christmas approaches, I am undecided as to exactly what type of jewelry would be to Ashley's liking as a second choice. I know what her first choice would be and am torn between emotion and common sense.

When I enter Bijoux Jewelers in downtown Boston, I look around as I stomp snow from my boots. I spot Corey Jacobson, a fellow graduate student from Farleigh. Corey is standing in front of a glass counter admiring the array of glistening engagement rings displayed before him. His brow is furrowed and from the look on his face, I can tell that he is in the midst of making a decision as to what size diamond to purchase. Yesterday, after class, Corey told me that he was going to propose to his steady, Heather Suthers, a former student at Farleigh. He said that she was scheduled for a visit the following weekend and that would be an ideal time to make the overture.

"Hey, Corey," I say, "having a tough time making a selection?"

Turning my direction, he smiles and says, "Hey, Grady." Then shaking his head, he adds, "My taste and my budget are as wide apart as the Grand Canyon. Don't want Heather to think I'm a cheapskate."

I walk over to the counter. The display of sparkling diamonds dazzles me. Slapping Corey on the shoulder, I say, "What's a few thousand dollars when it comes to a lifetime investment? Don't want Heather to be walking around with a trinket all your married life, do you? Remember, a man's success is judged by the size of the diamond on his wife's engagement ring."

Without responding to me, he picks up what I surmise is the most expensive of the two rings he was examining and hands it to the clerk, who says, "Good choice."

As the clerk replaces the ring tray under the glass counter and heads toward the register with Corey's selection, Corey turns to me and says, "It's always a 'good choice' in the eyes of the sales clerk when you purchase an item that is way overpriced and beyond your budget. The higher the commission, the higher the compliment." Corey reaches into his back pocket and pulls out his wallet. "Guess I better go sign my life away."

I watch Corey walk toward the register and then a diamond that stands out like the North Star draws my attention. It glistens in the showcase like none of the other diamonds, and I interpret that as a divine sign that Ashley's Christmas gift should not be a necklace, bracelet or set of earrings but an engagement ring! It was either now or never.

I'm still gazing at the diamond when Corey, holding a bright red gift bag adorned with green satin ribbon, approaches me on his way out and smiles.

Pointing to the bag and mimicking the clerk, I say, "Good choice."

"The girl or the ring?" he asks. I wonder if the same thing for myself.

• • •

Christmas Eve 1987. As I thumb through our family album, I retrieve the photograph of Ashley and me at her parents' home in Grand Junction. Standing in front of the lavishly decorated Colorado blue spruce, surrounded by mountains of gifts and discarded wrapping paper and bows, Ashley holds up her ring finger. Even in the decades old Polaroid the diamond sparkles.

When I look at Ashley's photograph in her stylish new ski outfit and see her patented sparkling turquoise eyes and radiant smile, I experience a feeling reminiscent of the feeling I had the moment we first met and the moment I proposed.

. . .

It was while we spent Christmas with Ashley's parents that we collaborated on our second musical composition, *You Taught Me*. We took turns on the Harden's baby grand piano composing the melody and making it fit the lyrics we had already written. I sang the first and last stanzas; Ashley sang the middle stanza. Our voices blended on the refrain and brought tears to both of our eyes.

Even years later when we sang *You Taught Me* to live audiences, we experienced the same sensation. We were told the band had virtually the same reaction. I don't remember a performance that didn't include, among our selections, **You Taught Me**. It spoke of the influence we had on each other and how our chance meeting would affect our lives forever.

> You taught me to reach for the stars
> To look beyond Mars
> To make tomorrow bright
>
> You taught me to set my sights high
> To reach for the sky
> To make everything right
> You taught me!
>
> *When you call, I will come*
> *When you speak, I will listen*
> *When you reach out, I will give you my heart*
> *All I know I learned from you*
> *In troubled times you saw me thru*
> *Yes, all I know I learned from you*
>
> You taught me not to wait for tomorrows

To set aside my sorrows
To make life a delight

You taught me to find many new ranges
To make many new changes
To search for the light
You taught me!

When you call, I will come
When you speak, I will listen
When you reach out, I will give you my heart
All I know I learned from you
In troubled times you saw me thru
Yes, all I know I learned from you

You taught me to forgive and forget
To make a sure bet
To fight with all my might

You taught me the meaning of love
To find heaven above
To never lose sight
You taught me!

When you call, I will come
When you speak, I will listen
When you reach out, I will give you my heart
All I know I learned from you
In troubled times you saw me thru
Yes, all I know I learned from you

• • •

My last semester at Farleigh was harried. I scurried to meet the demands of heavy bookings, establishing a recording studio, finishing comps, graduating, and preparing for an upcoming wedding. It was difficult to find the time and energy to do justice to each. "By juggling so many balls in the air at the same time, you're apt to drop some and maybe all," my father had said to me. "Don't spread yourself too thin," my mother had admonished. "Failure feeds on doing too much with too little."

I'd picked up a bad habit as a member of The New York Five that seemed to have escalated by my last year in graduate school. The genie in my bottle was vodka and it was not long before it became my constant companion. Soon, celebration became a way to cope. Drinking consumed me. But it had not yet begun to interfere with my studies or my relationship with Ashley. I considered it a performance-enhancing drug, not a weight that would drag me under. Besides, all musicians drank—a lot!

. . .

Over dinner at Cal's grill, on the eve of spring break our last year at Farleigh, Ashley surprises me when she announces she will not be spending spring break with me or her parents but rather on an excursion with her ex-high school classmates in Cancun.

I'm stunned. *She springs this on me the night before leaving for Cancun?* "But I thought…" I say and find myself at a loss for words, which for me is unusual.

"Oh, come on, Grady. It's my last hurrah before I settle down." Ashley pushes potato salad around with her fork. She looks at me and juts her chin defiantly. "And besides, all my friends are going and it may be the last time all of us will be together."

"I thought Cancun would be a good place to honeymoon," I say, hoping to lay a guilt trip on her for spoiling my plans and a cause to reconsider. My ruse doesn't work.

Ashley looks around the restaurant, and after a moment, she looks back at me. "Okay, I'll scope out the place while I'm there," she replies, without a hint of remorse for going without me. I suppose my hurt expression finally filters through to her. Her tone softens when she adds, "So we won't have unnecessary surprises when we spend our honeymoon there."

I'm insulted that she thinks throwing me the unnecessary surprises crumb would placate me. However, I'm not looking for a fight and try to salvage something, so I ask, "Wouldn't it be more fun for us to do it together?"

"Don't you understand, Grady? We'll have a whole lifetime to explore and have adventures together. This may be the last opportunity I'll have to romp with my high school buddies."

"Why spring break?" I lick my lips and look around. Cal's doesn't serve liquor and I find I'm suddenly needing a vodka Collins. As usual, Ashley is oblivious to my needs and presses on.

"It will be an early high school reunion and a good way to celebrate college graduation."

I'm now struggling with trying to get the genie back in the bottle. "How long will you be gone?"

"I'll spend five days in Cancun and the rest of spring break in Colorado with my parents."

I know my feelings don't matter when there's a conflict between what I want and what Ashley wants. Ashley always wins. I rein in my hurt and anger, and we finish dinner in virtual silence. When I drop Ashley off at the apartment complex, she barely brushes my cheek with a weak kiss. "Come on, Grady, don't look so glum. I'll be back before you know it."

Although we are standing there together, it feels as though she has already left.

• • •

I fly back to New York to spend spring break with my parents and to prepare for comps. After a few days, when I've not heard from Ashley, I call her parents.

"She's doing great and enjoying Cancun," her mother says.

"That's good." Then I seek confirmation. "Hear she's due back Saturday."

"That was the original plan, but apparently, some decided to stay over a few more days. Ashley revised her schedule and won't return until the following Wednesday."

My heart sinks. There's an awkward silence and I get the impression Mrs. Harden thought I knew. I should have known. *Why didn't Ashley have the decency to at least tell me herself?* I finally ask, "Think she'll be all right? Being gone for such a long period of time, I mean."

"Heavens, yes!" I detect relief in her voice; it appears we're back on safe ground. Mrs. Harden takes a deep breath and rushes on, "She went through grade school and high school with almost all of them. She's sharing a room with three of her best friends. One of them is Tina Richards, the daughter of our next-door neighbor. One of the young men is Brad Sessions, the son of one of the physicians in Tim's clinic and also one of our neighbors. In fact, Brad was Ashley's steady in high school."

That bit of information does little to comfort me.

• • •

While I was on Christmas break with Ashley and her parents in Colorado, like all proud parents, Ashley's mother had shown me Ashley's photo albums and year books. The pages were littered with pictures of Ashley: homecoming queen, student council president, captain of the cheerleading squad, valedictorian… Although I had not connected the dots then, I wondered why Ashley's date at the various high school proms seemed familiar. When I asked Ashley if the person pictured with her went to Farleigh, she said, "No, he's a pre-med student at Boston U." I'm certain that's the same man I saw Ashley with at the Boston Cosmopolitan Hotel the previous semester. The pieces of the puzzle slid together. Yet why would Ashley accept my marriage proposal if Brad was still in the picture?

• • •

When Ashley returns from spring break, I keep my suspicions to myself though I'm tempted to confront her with what I know, or what I think I know. Ashley will either deny or dodge the implications like she usually does. She has a knack for turning the tables and making me feel guilty for even questioning her loyalty. I will have gained nothing, and in the process, labeled myself possessive and paranoid.

• • •

If Ashley was double dealing, it was not readily apparent. Everything between us was as good or even better than before Ashley's trip to Cancun. The wedding plans occupied us and Ashley seemed excited about being Mrs. Grady Winslow.

I had pretty much made up my mind to look at the big picture and not be persuaded by pure supposition and take things out of context. *All may not be what it appears to be.* It was while in this frame of mind that I field a strange call from a person who does not wish to be identified.

"Is this Grady Winslow?" the female voice asks.

Thinking it might be a call from a solicitor, I flippantly respond, "Who's asking?"

"I can't tell you who I am, only that I spent spring break in Cancun with your fiancée."

"What's my fiancée's name?" Something close to terror seizes me. I know what's coming.

"Ashley Harden."

My knees become weak, and I sink down onto the sofa. Still trying to sound flippant, I manage to say, "What's this all about and why can't you give me your name?"

"Never mind. I'll be brief. Since you and I have something in common, I thought you should know. I'm an ex-classmate of Ashley's and have been dating her ex-boyfriend. In Cancun, the two spent a lot of time together and disappeared for long periods of time. They stayed in Cancun while the rest of us came home."

"If the two of you were a thing, how was it that your boyfriend abandoned you in favor of Ashley?"

"Almost as soon as we arrived in Cancun, Ashley told me my boyfriend didn't want to date me any longer and didn't have the heart to tell me. I was heartbroken, and to think he would confide in Ashley something that intimate, made it worse."

I rubbed my brow, confused, and frustrated. "I suppose she told your boyfriend the same thing?"

"How'd you know? When we compared notes later, he confirmed it."

"Sounds like the two of you may be back together. Are you?"

"We're working on it."

"Where do you live?" I ask, still hoping for a flaw in her version.

"Grand Junction, Colorado."

"What's the boyfriend's name?"

"Brad Sessions."

I wonder if this is the girl next door. "Your name wouldn't be Tina Richards, by chance, would it?"

The caller abruptly hung up. It didn't take the likes of a Sherlock Holmes to figure out the name of the caller. Just like that, I had the telling evidence and the confirmation I needed that my imagination was not running wild with me. It wasn't what I wanted to hear but what I suspected all along.

Suddenly all of the rationalizing I've done trying to convince myself that I'm paranoid as far as Ashley is concerned comes crashing down on me. Eyewitness testimony trumps supposition every time, and now with my greatest fears confirmed, I'm in a quandary. To break the engagement or not to break the engagement? That is the question. Although I love Ashley, I cannot tolerate infidelity. *If it's that way now, what's it going to be like when everything is humdrum?* I decide to wait and watch. In the interim, I call my father.

"Dad, Grady here."

I can hear the smile in Dad's voice as he says, "How's the boy wonder?"

"Bewildered."

"How so?" The smile in his voice is replaced with an element of concern.

"I heard from a reliable source that Ashley renewed an old friendship while in Cancun. The little birdie who told me is the old friend's girlfriend."

"Un-huh. So it appears you have firsthand information."

I sigh. "I played devil's advocate and tried really hard not to believe it, but the facts confirm her story. She's a victim of lies and deceit, too."

"But you and Ashley are engaged." I visualize Dad rubbing the stubble on his chin. "Can't imagine she would jeopardize the engagement with extra-curricular activities."

I have to smile at Dad's choice of words and naïveté in thinking that an engagement ring would alter Ashley's desire to engage in *extra-curricular activities*. "Unfortunately, she has. The ring is not the magic talisman I hoped it would be. Guess I should feel fortunate to be exposed to the reality *before* having taken the grand leap."

"Do I interpret that to mean you'll be calling off the engagement?"

"I'm leaning in that direction but thought I'd run it by you first."

"No doubt you have a tiger by the tail. But that comes with the territory. Someone like Ashley is bound to attract a lot of attention, much of it unwanted by either you or her. Then again, it brings up that age-old question: 'Do you want a gem everyone wants or a gem no one wants?' With Ashley on your arm, you'll need more than a flyswatter to keep those who envy you and covet Ashley away."

"Well, I'm beginning to realize that unwanted attention is not a one-way street. Ashley seems to relish in all the attention," I say. "In fact, she encourages it by flirting with every man she sees."

I'm beginning to think Dad just doesn't get it when he says, "Well, she could keep her attributes covered and venture out only in the shadows of night. Is that what you want?"

Wonder how he'd react if Mom acted like Ashley. "What I want is for her to act like my wife to be."

"To rebuff rather than induce, generate, or encourage. Is that what you mean?"

"Exactly!"

Sounds to me like Dad's enjoying this little tête-à-tête when he says, "In other words, you want a woman who is abrasive, nasty and abrupt—attributes that will drive men away instead of attracting them."

"Okay, so what you're saying is there is no middle ground," I say. "Funny. Other women can be congenial without having their words and manner interpreted as an invitation. Ashley goes out of her way to flirt and elicit sexual responses from the opposite sex. If it takes being abrasive, nasty and abrupt to ensure a monogamous relationship, then the answer is yes, that's how I want her." I hang up.

I pause a moment, then redial Dad's number.

"I've already given you my opinion," he says without even so much as a hello.

"That's cruel," I say, "I want my fiancée to be abrasive, nasty and abrupt, not my dad." I can hear him chuckle. "One more question. Is it insensitive of me to ask for the ring back?"

"Insensitive? Hell, no! Considering all she's put you through, I'm surprised that now you're worried about being insensitive! Besides, judging from the size of the diamond, I'd say you'd be foolish if you didn't."

• • •

After I hang up, I'm still at a loss. Though I can't remember a time when Ashley didn't control my every thought, there are times, more frequently now, that I wish I'd never met her. Sounds like my father is in the same quandary. Not sure my father is in favor of a breakup, only that if there is one I should ask for the ring back. I run my hands through my hair. Will I ever be rid of what I've now come to consider a curse?

As I mull everything over, still unsure of my next move, my mother calls.

"Grady, I just spoke to your father about calling off your engagement with Ashley." The urgency in her voice sets the tone.

"Though it is not my business, I feel compelled to add my two cents." Mom pauses for a few moments. "That is, if you're interested in hearing what I have to say."

I almost laugh; I've been pestering almost everyone I know with my dilemma. "Of course, I'm interested," I say, feeling guilty about not having involved her in my conversation with Dad in the first place. "I don't want to do something I'll be sorry for later."

"I've had my misgivings about Ashley from the start," Mom begins. "I didn't think it was my place to interfere." That's rich. Since when did Mom hold back? "But remember the summer Ashley spent with us, you and I had a long conversation about the incident that took place the first night we all dined out?"

"Yes, you and Dad took Ashley and me to the San Marco Room at the Palace Arms Hotel. I was upset with Ashley and cried on your shoulder." Yes, I remember it well and am still embarrassed by the way I reacted.

"In retrospect, I gave you bad advice. I told you it was natural to be possessive and that by being possessive it showed you cared." Mom pauses. "However, son, I've revised my position. I think Ashley intentionally flaunts these other encounters to make you jealous and then goes out of her way to put you on the defensive. She knows which buttons to push, and you, poor boy, play right into her hand. She absolutely wants you to know there's many, many other fish in the sea, and if you don't like it, lump it."

"Yes, and I remember you saying to stick it out and that trust was implicit in any lasting relationship."

"And I have to admit that was bad advice. I never shared with you how much it bothered me when Ashley left me stranded while she flirted with the maître d' on our return trip from the powder room."

"She returned with the name and telephone number of the maître d' scribbled on the back of a business card. Remember the look on his face when I called the maître d' by his first name when we left?"

"I remember the look on *your* face when Ashley dropped the card, and you picked it up and discovered the name and number on the back. I was thankful you didn't make more of a scene. Grady, you're our only child and your happiness means everything to Dad and me."

"I know, Mom. I'm trying to work it out. The thing that bothered me was Ashley's nonchalant attitude. She just reached for the card and placed it in her purse as if it was an everyday occurrence."

"Maybe it is," Mom says and repeats, "maybe it is."

As we discuss Ashley and the chances that our relationship will survive, and considering Ashley's checkered past, I'm more convinced than ever that married life with Ashley would be a revolving door.

"You can't change her; you're the only person you can change. Be patient, Grady, you'll find the right one. And when you do, you'll know it."

Mom's words echo in my head. "You can't change her. You're the only person you can change."

• • •

Since I apparently don't have the ability to make a decision, I'm still looking for advice and a solution to my dilemma. Charlie has always given it to me straight with little regard for my feelings, so I decide to confide in him.

I pull Charlie aside before rehearsal, and after I bare my soul to him, he says, "Sorry, buddy, we've had this talk several times. Standing on the outside looking in I could see it coming. Why not just put everything on hold and let nature take its course? Why rush into anything when you don't have to? Deliberation is better than regret!"

"How do I break the news to Ashley?"

Charlie guffaws. "You afraid of hurting her feelings? Get real. She doesn't have any."

• • •

Early that Thursday when I arrive at our practice session, I'm surprised that the band has started without Ashley and me.

"Hey, Grady, we have a number we want you to hear before Ashley arrives," Charlie says.

"Okay," I'm apprehensive and sit down at the piano not knowing what to expect.

After a brief overture, the band plays and sings what they call ***Before It's Too Late.***

> Most of us have been there sometime in our life
> We know the struggle; have experienced the strife
> We watch our friend wrestle with what to do
> Ah! It's a shame what women can do to you

The rest of the band sings the refrain:

> *Drop her, ditch her, dump her, pitch her*
> *Give her the gate before it's too late*

Freddie sings the next verse:

> Take our advice, she's not very nice
> She'll use you up and when she's through
> She's the one that'll dump you
> Women like that always do

Again, the rest of the band sings the refrain:

> *Drop her, ditch her, dump her, pitch her*
> *Give her the gate before it's too late*

Denny then sets aside his sax and sings:

> Listen to us, she'll tear you apart and
> She doesn't care if she breaks your heart
> She doesn't know how to give, just takes
> Come on, Grady, we all make mistakes

Again, the rest of the band sings the refrain:

> *Drop her, ditch her, dump her, pitch her*

Give her the gate before it's too late

Charlie then sings the last verse:

> Drop her, ditch her, dump her, pitch her
> Toss her, cross her, give her the gate
> Wake up, Grady, before it's too late
> There's lots of fish in the sea
> She's not the only one, soon you'll see

We're not sure at which point in the rendition Ashley arrives. When we hear her mock applause at the conclusion of the last verse, we all turn in her direction.

She saunters across the platform in my direction. When she reaches the piano, she nudges me over and positions herself in front of the keyboard. Adjusting the mic, she begins to play and sing what she calls **Moments In Time**.

> Grady, you know I can't help being me
> Can't be the person you want me to be
> So what if I like attention from men
> It's a normal reaction, it's not a sin
>
> *These other flings are just moments in time*
> *You're the one I love, you'll always be mine*
>
> Don't judge me, you haven't the right
> I just can't stand it when we fight
> If you loved me you'd understand
> Things just happen, they're not planned
>
> *These other flings are just moments in time*
> *You're the one I love, you'll always be mine*
>
> Don't degrade me, I won't be mocked
> If you cage me, I'll pick the lock
> Need to live my life; need to be free

I'll just die if you stifle me
These other flings are just moments in time
If you can't understand, then you'll never be mine

As quickly and unobtrusively as she arrives, she leaves. I rise and head in her direction. Charlie steps in front of me, plants his palm firmly against my chest, and says, "Let her go. Give her time to cool. She'll be all right."

· · ·

Determined not to make the next move, I don't contact Ashley. She didn't show for our Friday performance at the Cosmo, so we schedule Jenny Doyle for Saturday and bill our group as Jenny and The New York Five.

Midweek, I receive a message from Ashley. "I'm waving the white flag," the message says. "If you're willing to bury the hatchet, give me a call."

That same day, before I can return the call, I run into Ashley at the student union.

"Are you still speaking to me?" she asks, and for the first time since meeting Ashley, she seems timid. I'm almost happy that the shoe is finally on the other foot.

Wanting to postpone the inevitable, I say, "We need to talk."

"I have time now," she says, and I detect a hint of hope in her voice.

"Dunkin' Donuts is across the way." I take her backpack from her shoulder. "That would be more private than the SU."

On our way, we engage in small talk and when we arrive at Dunkin' Donuts, Ashley grabs a booth. As I stand in line waiting to purchase coffee and donuts, I glance back at her. She is twisting the engagement ring on her finger as she stares out the window.

"Didn't know whether you wanted coconut or chocolate," I say, as I set the tray down on the table, "so I got one of each."

"Thank you," she says, avoiding eye contact. She doctors her coffee with cream and sugar.

"Anxious for finals?" I ask.

"Finals, no; graduation, yes." When she looks up I see apprehension in her eyes.

I slide the tray in her direction. She selects coconut. As I take a bite out of the chocolate donut, I sense tension developing between us. I'm not sure if her apprehension is school-related or because of me and what it is she thinks I have to say. After an awkward moment, I say, "You seem preoccupied. Hope I'm not the cause."

Ashley slowly stirs her coffee, and without looking up, says, "I'll have to admit you're a distraction. Guess my life is in flux and my future a total mystery." She finally looks at me and says, "Sounds as though you want to break our engagement."

"Why do you say that?" I'm caught off guard when she brings up the subject.

"Call it a woman's intuition. I've sensed something is not quite right between us since I came back from spring break. It's obvious something is bothering you." She sets the partially eaten donut aside and glares at me.

If looks could kill I'd be six feet under. "Heard some rumors," I say and dab at my mouth with a napkin.

"Like what?" she demands, pushing her coffee cup back away from her, still glaring at me.

This scenario is all too familiar. It sounds like she's reversing our roles and trying to put me on the ropes. Not gonna happen. Maybe the old me, but not now. Recrimination has always been her best weapon.

She must have recognized the determination written on my face. "Looks like you're just looking for an excuse to breakup," she says defiantly.

"Not really," I reply. "I'm just confused. One moment you tell me you love me. The next minute you act as though I'm the plague." As always, when I'm in her presence I have difficulty getting to the heart of the matter for obvious reasons. If I was wrong about Ashley, and I hoped I was, I didn't want to cut off a retreat route. Yet I knew I had to confront her with the evidence of her infidelity. I stand my ground.

"I don't know what you're talking about," she says and shrugs.

Her matter-of-fact attitude pushes me to the edge. I blurt, "Your romantic interlude with Brad Sessions during spring break, for one!" I say, holding up a finger, then I raise a second finger and snap, "Causing the breakup of Brad and his girlfriend and then latching onto Brad, for another. Do you want me to go on?" I'm on agitation overload at this point. I watch for a chink to appear in Ashley's armor. No such luck.

She must have finally realized she wasn't in a position to argue. In true Ashley fashion, when she hasn't a leg to stand on, she retreats. Tossing her napkin onto the table, she stands and hisses, "I've heard enough!" and starts to walk away.

"Wait." I rub my forehead not sure what to say next. I don't want to create a scene.

She doesn't miss a beat. "Haven't you said enough already?" She glares at me and crosses her arms.

I'm angry and hurt and can't hide it. "I think you owe me an explanation!"

Ashley comes back, and leaning forward, places both hands on the table. "I owe you nothing!" With that, she stands erect and jerks the engagement ring off her finger and plants it in my hand. "There! Hope you're satisfied!" She stomps away, grumbling. I slink away when the din in the coffee shop turns to whispers and all eyes are focused on the two of us.

• • •

I am surprised when Freddie tells me some days later that a sheriff's deputy is looking for me. He hands me a card with the deputy's name and telephone number. I dial the number.

"Suffolk County Sheriff's Department, Deputy Brodie speaking."

"This is Grady Winslow, Deputy Brodie. I'm a graduate student at Farleigh and understand you were trying to contact me."

I can hear the shuffling of papers. "Have a civil summons to serve on you. I can either bring it out to you or you can stop by the Suffolk County Sheriff's Department and pick it up. Your call."

"I'll come pick it up," I say. I don't want a uniformed sheriff's deputy coming to our apartment building, causing a stir. I wasn't sure what it was all about, only grateful it was not an arrest warrant. "My last class gets out at around three-thirty. Can I pick it up then?"

"I should be here, but if I'm not, just speak to the clerk and someone else will provide service."

• • •

When I arrive at the Suffolk County Sheriff's Department, a burly sheriff's deputy spots me. "I'm here to pick up a summons from Deputy Brodie," I say. "He's expecting me."

"Grady Winslow?"

"One and the same," I reply and shake Deputy Brodie's hand.

"Wait here," he says and goes down the hall to another room. When he comes back, he hands me two documents. One is a summons; the other, a complaint.

I'm stunned. "What's all of this mean?"

"The summons advises you that a civil action has been filed against you and that, if you don't respond within the time specified, judgment will be entered against you. The complaint, in layman terms, alleges you have certain property in your possession belonging to an Ashley Harden and she wants it back."

"Good God!" I exclaim. "My ex-fiancée wants her engagement ring back."

Deputy Brodie just shrugs and bites his bottom lip. No sympathy there.

"Do I have to give back the ring?" I ask.

"Depends," Deputy Brodie says and then quickly adds, "Of course, that's something you will need to discuss with an attorney."

"Do I have to hire an attorney?"

"If you don't want to give the ring back."

"And if I give back the ring, am I re-engaged?"

Deputy Brodie laughs.

• • •

When I call my father and describe the predicament, he advises me to hire a lawyer and agrees to pay the fees. He says he will speak to our family attorney and get a referral.

Less than thirty minutes later my father is back on the phone.

"I just talked to Payton Dreyden. He recommended you get in touch with Roy Sheridan at Sheridan, Porter & Mansfield in Boston. He apparently went to law school with Mr. Sheridan and says he is an AV rated attorney, the highest rating an attorney can achieve, and one he would hire if he were in trouble."

"Am I in trouble?"

"You would be if you married a woman like Ashley. It's fortunate you didn't get married and *then* find out what she's like."

"Did you talk to Peyton about my chances of winning or losing?"

"He said if you were in Colorado when you presented Ashley with the ring, it would be considered a conditional gift and the donor, namely you, would get it back. He wasn't sure what the law is in Massachusetts. In some states it's dependent on who was at fault in breaking the engagement. If the donor was not at fault, he would get the ring back. If the done, namely Ashley, was at fault, she would have to return it. In other states, like Montana, Peyton said it would be considered an unconditional gift and Ashley could keep the ring regardless of whether the marriage took place or not. Peyton also said that since the ring was given to Ashley in Colorado, Colorado law should apply."

"But I already have the ring. Ashley returned it."

"Payton said that was in your favor. Even in a fault state, according to Payton, it wouldn't make any difference who was at fault since the donee returned it. In other words, regardless of whether you requested that it be returned or had broken the engagement, her voluntary relinquishment, at least according to Peyton, would be considered a waiver."

"Would I be better off if I just gave the damn thing back?"

"For twelve thousand dollars and the principle, you'd be a fool to do it. If you fold, she'll consider you weak. Stand up like the man that you are, and as they said when I was in the Army, 'Take no prisoners.' Besides, it looks like the law is in your favor."

• • •

As I was escorted to Roy Sheridan's private office, I was having misgivings about opposing Ashley, especially in a courtroom. It was obvious from the trappings that Sheridan, Porter & Mansfield was one of Massachusetts' premier law firms. In no time, it was also obvious that Roy Sheridan was the kind of lawyer I wanted on my side.

"In Massachusetts," he says, "the giving and acceptance of an engagement ring is considered a conditional gift. The donee ordinarily is required to return the ring if the engagement is broken. However, in Massachusetts, an engagement ring given on a birthday or on Christmas might be considered an unconditional gift if the court determines the ring was a birthday or Christmas gift. Even if the court applies Colorado law, the outcome would, in all likelihood, still be the same."

"Since I gave the ring to Ashley on Christmas day, I assume she will be awarded the ring."

"Not necessarily. The law is pretty clear, at least in my eyes, that the voluntary return of the ring by Ashley is dispositive of the issue. Notice I said 'voluntary.' She may argue she was coerced into returning the ring and that doing so was *not* a free and voluntary act on her part. That's the ringer, to borrow a cliché. If the court finds evidence of duress or coercion, she wins. Otherwise, you win."

Despite holding the aces, my misgivings about mounting a defense had more to do with loyalty than anything else. To oppose Ashley was like opposing my mother. It was not in my DNA.

• • •

After the answer to the complaint was filed, I received a number of threatening telephone calls. All were from pay phones in downtown Boston. Ashley also mailed me the severed head of a teddy bear that I had given her. On one occasion, someone keyed the driver's side of my Chevy Malibu. So much for litigator's remorse.

• • •

Since Ashley would be graduating in May, she requested that our case be advanced on the court's docket. I didn't oppose her request.

• • •

"Would you state your full name?"

"Tamara Ashley Harden."

"Do you go by a nickname?"

"I go by my middle name Ashley."

"What is your occupation?"

"I'm a senior at Farleigh College of Music here in Boston."

"Were you a member of a band known as Ashley and The New York Five?"

"Yes."

Was one of the members of the band a graduate student at Farleigh by the name of Grady Winslow?"

"Yes. However, I had known Grady just prior to joining the band."

"Do you see that same man in court?"

"Yes, he's the man seated at the defendant's table with the blue blazer," Ashley then points in my direction.

"Did you subsequently develop a romantic relationship with Grady?"

"Yes."

"Did that lead to a marriage proposal and Grady presenting you with an engagement ring?"

"Yes."

"Is that the one and the same ring that is the subject of this law suit?"

"Yes."

"When Grady presented you with the ring, did he say anything?"

"That he loved me and wanted to marry me."

"Did you accept the ring and the proposal?"

"Yes. I told him yes and that I loved him."

"When he presented the ring, did he mention that it was conditioned upon marriage?"

"No. I considered it an outright gift primarily because it was given to me on Christmas Day."

"Did there come a time when Grady wanted the ring back?"

"He didn't come right out and say that but that was my interpretation."

"What happened?"

"Shortly after I returned from spring break, the band had a practice session which started before my arrival. When I arrived, they were singing a song suggesting that Grady dump me."

"Did there come a time when you learned why the band was suggesting such a thing?"

"Yes."

"By the way, was the song aimed at your affiliation with the band or as Grady's fiancée?"

"I interpreted it to be as Grady's fiancée."

"At what point did you arrive at the practice session?"

"Just as they were beginning the song suggesting that Grady dump me."

"Was Grady participating in the song?"

"No, he was just observing as was I."

"Did Grady do anything to indicate whether he either agreed or disagreed with what was being suggested?"

"Not that I could tell."

"After the song concluded what did you do?"

"I made my presence known by walking across the stage and nudging Grady to the edge of the bench in front of the keyboard. I then played an improvised song with lyrics professing my love for

Grady and my apologizes for making his life so miserable."

"What did you do next?"

"I walked out of the room and out of the band because of the perceived rejection."

"Did Grady try to stop you?"

"No."

"Did there come a time when Grady gave you an explanation as to why he was upset with you?"

"Yes. Approximately a week later, I ran into him at the Farleigh student union and we walked across the street and had coffee at a restaurant. He said he had something he wanted to talk about."

"While at coffee, did he confide in you as to the reason he was upset?"

"When I asked Grady what was bothering him and whether he was having second thoughts about marrying me, he accused me basically of having an affair with an ex-boyfriend of mine by the name of Brad Sessions. He also accused me of orchestrating the breakup of Brad with Brad's then girlfriend."

"Did you respond?"

"I didn't want to dignify the accusations and started to walk away. Before doing so, I removed the ring from my finger and gave it to Grady."

"When you handed him the ring, did you say anything?"

"Only that I hoped he was satisfied."

"Did he say or do anything?"

"Not that I saw or heard."

"What did you do next?"

"I just walked away in tears."

"Did you want to break up with Grady?"

"No!"

"Why did you give the ring back?"

"Because I thought that was what he wanted."

Ashley played the part of the rejected lover to perfection. Even

I was starting to feel sorry for her. Her attorney, Lowell Cambridge, had prepared her well. Cambridge had an athletic build and movie-star good looks. According to Mr. Sheridan, Cambridge was a transplant from California and his list of former clients included a number of starlets and sports figures. The mystery was not *why* Ashley hired him but *how* Ashley was paying him for his services.

When it was Mr. Sheridan's turn to cross-examine Ashley, I requested that he be gentle.

"I never badger witnesses. I will lace my examination with kindness," he murmured as he rose.

"Miss Harden," Mr. Sheridan began, "Farleigh College of Music is also my wife's *alma mater*. You are graduating from a fine institution."

Ashley managed a smile but did not reply.

"I take it everything was going smoothly between you and Grady up to the time you left for spring break. Is that correct?"

"What do you mean up to the time I left for spring break?"

"When you and Grady said your goodbyes immediately prior to your departure at spring break, you weren't wearing your engagement ring, were you?"

"No. The night before Grady and I had a spat and I removed it."

"Was that because the night before you were scheduled to leave on spring break, you sprang on him your plan not to spend spring break with him or your family but instead spend it with your high school classmates in Cancun?"

"Partly."

"If the roles had been reversed, wouldn't you have been upset also?"

"I don't know."

"An engagement ring is not something you obtain in a Cracker Jack box but a symbol of lasting love between the donor when it is given and the donee when it is accepted and worn. Isn't that true?"

"I guess so."

"Grady didn't ask you to remove the engagement ring before you left on spring break or after you returned, did he?"

"Not by word but by action."

"So, by not being happy about you changing your plans the last minute and not spending spring break with him and your parents, his action, at least in your eyes, was tantamount to him asking you to remove your engagement ring?"

"Yes. By accusing me or at least implying that I had an affair with my ex-boyfriend in Cancun and being the cause of Brad's breakup with his then girlfriend was tantamount to Grady asking me to remove the engagement ring."

"By the way, Miss Harden, only you and your ex-boyfriend extended your stay in Cancun and were the only two to stay behind, am I right?"

Ashley just glared at Mr. Sheridan. "Yes," she whispered.

"And by Grady's reaction to your last-minute decision to spend spring break in Cancun and his so-called accusations, you interpreted them to mean Grady wanted to break off the engagement and for you to give back the ring?"

"Yes."

"So then, Miss Harden, would it be fair to say Grady never verbally asked you to remove the engagement ring and return it?"

"I guess you might say that."

"He never physically took the ring from you, did he?"

"No."

"You removed the ring from your finger and planted it in his hand as a final gesture of the termination of your engagement, didn't you?"

Ashley stayed silent.

The judge said, "Please answer the question, Ms. Harden."

She fidgeted before answering, "Yes."

Mr. Sheridan scanned his notes and came over to where I was sitting and asked if he'd missed anything. I shook my head.

"I have no further questions, Your Honor."

"Any other evidence to present?" the judge asked Mr. Cambridge.

"Nothing further," Cambridge responded.

"This would be a good place to take a recess," the judge said. And to Mr. Sheridan, he said, "Be prepared to present your defense."

• • •

Since there was no disagreement over the facts, it boiled down to an interpretation of the law. Mr. Sheridan opted not to call me as a witness or put on any evidence. His argument to the court was sweet and simple.

"Your Honor, whether we apply Colorado or Massachusetts law, by returning the gift, the intended donee, here the Plaintiff, symbolically rejected it. One of the requirements of a gift is that it be accepted. Here it was rejected. Plaintiff, having failed to prove her claim by a preponderance of the evidence, cannot prevail. Judgment must, therefore, be entered in favor of the Defendant."

Cambridge's argument that the return was coerced fell on deaf ears. The judge ruled in our favor. Surprisingly, Ashley showed no reaction. In fact, when she left the courtroom, she flashed me a broad smile.

The one thing predictable about Ashley was her unpredictability.

CHAPTER NINE

How Can I Tell You

GRADY

Graduation day 1987 was more than a May or *maybe* day. It represented a day of completion and achievement. Ashley received her B.A. degree in Jazz Composition and Arranging; I received my M.M. degree in Music Composition and Classical Contemporary Music Performance. I reverently studied my diploma. Six years of my life were represented on that one piece of parchment. It was while at graduation that I learned that Ashley would be pursuing her M.M. degree at Farleigh.

Lest I jump ahead too rapidly, let me relate the nature of my relationship with Ashley following the court case. In a word, *nonexistent*. It wasn't until the reception following graduation that we even spoke to each other. I wasn't surprised when Ashley showed up with Brad. Yes, the same Brad that caused the breakup. Guess Ashley couldn't help rubbing my nose in it. Jenny Doyle accompanied me and had taken over where Ashley had left off both in the band and in my heart.

I was too elated to stay glum for long, so I put on my happy face determined not to let Ashley ruin this very special day in my life. Surprisingly enough, Ashley and I were civil to each other. While Ashley's parents and grandfather visited with my mother and father, Ashley and Brad visited with Jenny and me. I would describe the evening as strained but not too uncomfortable. It was refreshing to be in Ashley's presence and not be intimidated by her.

Ashley's parents and mine seemed to enjoy each other's company despite the breakup. They spent a lot of time together at the reception while the graduates mingled. I learned later from my parents that our two families planned a vacation in Spain together. Dad was scheduled for an international concert tour culminating with a performance in Valencia in mid-August. Dad told me later that he volunteered to make the reservations for both families at the Valencia International Hotel near the concert hall where he was scheduled to perform. When I pulled up a map, I discovered Valencia was located on the southeastern coast of Spain where the Turia River meets the Mediterranean Sea. Although I had been to Madrid and Barcelona years before, I didn't remember ever being in Valencia, a beautiful city known for its arts and sciences.

• • •

At the beginning of my second semester in graduate school, having developed a taste and aptitude for classical music, I had added Classical Contemporary Music Performance to my area of concentration. My father was most pleased, and by that time, I had begun playing duets with him at several of his concerts. On occasion, I would play a solo. He claimed I was a natural and I seemed to gravitate toward classical. *Who would have thought?*

The summer after graduation I stayed at Winslow Mansion with my parents and accompanied my father on his world concert tours helping with the arrangements and performances and being a part of the program. Touring with my father was an experience I'd treasure for the rest of my life. We bonded, and as an adult, I began seeing Dad with different eyes. On occasion, we arranged for Jenny and her parents to be our guests. During this period, I had no contact with Ashley.

• • •

Performing before great crowds worldwide and having to make repeated curtain calls was an elixir. The New York Five performances didn't come close to the high I got from performing before international audiences on the world stage. With Ashley no longer the center of my life, I could concentrate on other things. Even alcohol no longer whetted my appetite, and I had a brighter outlook on life.

Whether anyone else noticed my transformation or not, I was keenly aware and had to smile every time I looked in the mirror knowing my future was for the taking. I was no longer dreaming an impossible dream or chasing a rainbow named Ashley. A bleak destiny no longer beckoned.

Summer was quickly ending, as was our European tour. Last stop was Valencia, Spain. I was no longer a token performer. It was obvious Dad considered me concert ready. With the privilege came the expectations and the stress. The many hours of practice were beginning to take their toll. As the weightlifters and runners say, "no pain, no gain." And to my credit, I stayed away from the booze. I actually enjoyed putting myself through the paces, testing my mettle, so to speak.

Mom accompanied Dad and me to Valencia where Ashley's parents were to meet us. We arrived on Monday, August twenty-fourth, four days ahead of our first scheduled performance. We were not booked to fly back to the states until Monday of the following week, the day after my twenty-fourth birthday.

• • •

When we arrive at the Valencia Airport in Manises on Wednesday, August twenty-sixth, the deplaning passengers of the Harden flight are already waiting in the baggage claim area. As the carousel begins to revolve, out of the corner of my eye I catch a glimpse of Ashley waving and attempting to attract my attention. She is with her parents, Dr. Timothy and Roslyn Harden. *OMG!* Didn't know Ashley would be with them.

Ashley lit up the baggage area with her stylish outfit, one usually found in glamour magazines. It's not outlandish in the least and shows just enough of her attributes to make it interesting. Her healthy tan and her radiant smile and sparkling turquoise eyes seem to attract the admiration of both locals and tourists alike. I'd forgotten how beautiful Ashley was. If only she was as beautiful on the inside!

Seeing her stirs up hurtful memories and my vindictive side wants to say, "What, no Brad!" Instead, I ask, "What are you doing here? I thought you were back in Boston."

"Finished summer school and am here to help you celebrate your birthday." After a pause, she adds, "Thought you might be happy to see me." It's then that I notice disappointment in her eyes.

I'm speechless. I finally manage to say, "What a nice surprise." In some ways I mean it. My heart beats with excitement as we embrace. Just the feel of her makes me realize how much I missed her.

She says what I'm thinking, "God, how I missed you!"

The next morning, as our parents finish their coffee, Ashley and I go down to the beach. As we carry our sandals and let the tide lick our feet and legs, she loops her arm through mine, and we find ourselves as we were pre-spring break when there was just Ashley and me.

At our rehearsal on Thursday, Ashley is present with Dad and me. She is wild with excitement as Dad and I play our duets.

"Ashley must be your talisman," Dad whispers midway through the rehearsal.

"What do you mean?" I whisper back.

"You've never played like this before. You're putting not only your heart, but your soul into the music."

"Guess you're right. That's because Ashley has never been present at any of our rehearsals or concerts before."

"If she's the cause, then she needs to be present at our concerts this weekend and every weekend. How many curtain calls are you willing to endure?"

I'm not surprised at Dad's reaction. Despite Ashley's and my topsy-turvy relationship, he's always liked her. "As many as possible; as many as possible," I reply. "I want to break the record."

Dad laughs. "That's my boy!"

After we rehearse our last number, Ashley applauds. Then she approaches and asks to use my piano. I oblige.

She produces a couple of pages of folded sheet music from her purse, and as she smooths the folds, she looks at me and says, "I composed a song for a class project, but I wrote it just for you. It's called *How Can I Tell You*.

Ashley gracefully slips onto the piano bench and smiles up at me. She begins by playing an intro and when she sings the lyrics, our eyes entangle. I am mesmerized by the words and enchanted by Ashley's charm. I fight to keep from falling back deeply and madly in love. I put my feelings on hold and just savor the message.

> How can I tell you
> What a difference you've made in my life
> How can I show you
> That I love you with all of my might
>
> How can I prove to you
> Exactly the way that I feel
> How can I convince you
> My commitment to you is real
>
> *Oh, what can I say*
> *What can I do*
> *You know I love you*
> *Without you I'm blue*
> *Take my hand and hold it tight*
> *Everything is going to be all right*
>
> How can I tell you
> How much joy you bring to me each day
> How can I show you
> That my love for you is here to stay
>
> How can I prove to you
> That nothing could ever change my mind
> How can I convince you
> That no matter you'll always be mine

Oh, what can I say
What can I do
You know I love you
Without you I'm blue
Take my hand and hold it tight
Everything is going to be all right
How can I tell you
Everything is going to be all right

The lyrics to Ashley's song move me and once again I'm caught in that trap despite my vow never to go there again.

• • •

Upon arrival in New York after our concert tour, I receive a call offering me a full professorship at Farleigh. I jump at the chance. My parents are not too enamored with the idea. "It sounds more like an excuse to be with Ashley than to teach," my father says.

My mother is more assertive, "Grady," she says, "Be prepared for another rollercoaster ride if you hook up with Ashley. She's just not the right girl for you!"

CHAPTER TEN

A Time to Remember

GRADY

By a twist of fate, my first assignment outside the classroom is to be in charge of the orientation program and the reception that follows for the M.M. students at Farleigh College of Music (FCM). I'm apprehensive about taking on the task. To teach and perform is not daunting. However, rhetoric is not my forte and I feel I have to be glib to prove my worth. Since music is my best mode of communication, and Farleigh is a music conservatory *par excellence*, it's only natural I would make one of my compositions the focal point of the evening.

Although composition usually came easy, I had a difficult time formulating the ideal lyrics and melody which would ultimately define my legacy at Farleigh. My composition would be scrutinized by the elite, and I would be judged harshly by friend and foe alike. With trepidation I undertook what turned out to be a nerve-racking experience—at least at the beginning.

I spent several sleepless nights and many agonizing hours at the piano before it came to me. I christened my composition *A Time To Remember*. The lyrics were structured to be timeless and endure graduation. They went like this:

> When I see the glint of snow
> And the evening stars that glow
> Feel a cool ocean breeze
> Or hear the rustle of leaves
>
> *I can't help but think of my youth*
> *A time too long ago*

When I was young and carefree

I picture white capped waves
Music laden fun-filled days
Feel the fresh Massachusetts air
And stare at clouds without care
Watch our college campus grow
Skinny dipping; freezing snow
My first date; coming home late

I can't help but think of my youth
A time too long ago
When I was young and carefree

Beacon Hill and Copley Square
The happy times we spent there
Walking down the Freedom Trail
Watching ships as they set sail
Boston Pops at Concert Hall
Shopping at Commonwealth Mall
Watching the Red Sox play baseball

I can't help but think of my youth
A time too long ago
When I was young and carefree

Where music reaches the sea
And enchantment seems to be
Is our college of Farleigh
Located in Boston, Mass
A school with lots of class
No place I'd rather be
If only I'd win the lottery

Ours was a time to remember
A time forever unto its own

• • •

When Ashley and I returned to Boston, we explored the possibility of reconciliation. Mainly at my insistence, we agreed to give each other time and space before making a commitment. Ashley seemed okay with the arrangement. I knew she and Brad were still seeing each other and she knew Jenny and I had not completely severed our ties. My common sense led me in one direction; my heart tugged in the opposite direction.

The reception for the M.M. students proves to be a litmus test in more ways than one. The recording I had made of *A Time To Remember* receives acclaim from even the most discerning and sets the tone, not just for the evening, but ultimately my full tenure at Farleigh.

As the song plays, I observe Ashley's reaction. She appears emotional and ultimately leaves the room briefly before the song has been concluded. When she returns, her eyes are riveted on me.

At the conclusion of the event, Ashley makes her way to where I'm standing, and pulling me aside, says, "We must talk! Meet me at my apartment."

Later that evening when I arrive at Ashley's apartment, she pulls me inside and greets me with a warm embrace and a passionate kiss. Even though we make it a point of avoiding the intimate relationship we had in the past, it wasn't long before we're making up for lost time and engaging in our favorite pastime.

For a few hours, I'm lost in that world that is all our own and having Ashley next to me feels familiar, comfortable, and right. I ignore the images that dance across my memory. *Just maybe we can make it work this time.*

After I get my breath back, I ask, "What about Brad?"

"What about him?" Ashley responds as she snuggles close.

"I thought things were serious between the two of you."

"No more than you and Jenny."

She didn't really answer my question, so I followed it up with,

"How do you know I'm not in love with Jenny?"

Tracing circles on my chest with her fingernail, she replies, "I know your heart."

"Am I that transparent?" I ask, surprised by my comment considering my vow not to become involved once again with someone who has a tendency to break hearts.

"You don't have to say anything. Your actions speak louder than words ever could."

"Sure, are you?"

"A woman knows when a man is in love with her and can't live without her."

"Lyrics straight out of *Can't Live Without You!*"

"A song you wrote just for me! It, of course, is the smoking gun."

"I plead guilty." Again, I'm dumbfounded at my inability to hide my feelings and struggle to stifle the urge to resurrect the unrelenting love I have deep down for her. She can read me like a book!

She pulls away from me. "Are you afraid to tell me you love me?"

"I thought you said I didn't have to say anything," I pull her back to me.

"I want you to tell me." I sense desperation in her voice.

I cave in. "Ashley, I could love no other as I love you."

The relief in her tone is evident. "Sounds like the opening lyrics of a new song."

• • •

I will dispense with the boring details of my breakup with Jenny. From what Ashley said, she and I had much the same experience when we told Jenny and Brad we were back together. We both were told in no uncertain terms that we were insensitive and narcissistic. Those were the repeatable words. Suffice it to say, we were immediately deleted from their Christmas card lists. Guess we expected as much. Our announcement came with little warning.

I don't know about Ashley's parents but mine are not completely enamored when I break the news that Ashley and I are back together.

"It's not as though we don't like Ashley," my father begins.

"It's just that we don't want to see you hurt again," my mother interjects.

"I understand," I reassure them. "I'm a big boy and fully realize the consequences of resuming the relationship. Nothing is ever certain, and if we could predict the future, we'd never make any mistakes."

"Walk before you run, son," Dad warns. "Impulsivity is an enemy, not a friend. And in your case, you don't always use sound judgment. So tread carefully!"

"I realize I don't have a great track record, especially when it comes to her," I confess. "But as one of my professors used to say, 'I may be wrong, but I'm not in doubt.'" I didn't mean to be disrespectful, only assertive. Believing it takes two to make it and two to break it; I feel I have better than a fifty-fifty chance to make it with Ashley.

• • •

I went home over Thanksgiving break, alone.

"What, no Ashley?" Dad asks as he meets me at JFK International.

"I told you Ashley would be spending the week in Colorado with her parents skiing in Steamboat."

"Your mother and I prepared for her arrival—just in case," Dad says with a tinge of disappointment in his voice.

"I thought you and Mom didn't approve of her." I step up and grab my duffel from the revolving Delta carrousel.

"The problem is we're not the only ones who think she's charming and desirable," Dad says, "and for those reasons feel your insecurity may not be totally unwarranted." He leads the way to the exit, and turning says, "There is some reluctance on our part to become attached to Ashley knowing the relationship may not endure."

"Dad, competition is not all that bad. It keeps me on my toes and makes me be all that I can be. As Mrs. Schaffer used to say, after her husband had been away on unexplained absences, 'Despite the shopping spree, he always returns to me!'"

"Come on, Grady, I know you don't believe that." Skepticism creeps into Dad's voice as he continues. "Nor do I think you would put up with it. I sure as hell wouldn't, and for that matter, don't know of anyone else who would. With you being so possessive, I think if you caught Ashley in bed with another man that would be the end of them."

"There are plenty of other fish in the sea. Some are worth keeping and others aren't. Why ruin your life over the one that's not a keeper?" I retort.

Dad laughs. "That's nonsense. With Ashley's propensity to flirt with every male that ogles her, I'm not sure that's how you'd feel if and when the time came," Dad says, as he opens the trunk and tosses my duffel inside. "I've seen how you've reacted, and so has your mother, when Ashley makes you jealous. And I don't think it's all so innocent and inadvertent as Ashley would have you believe. She seems to delight in your discomfort and goes out of her way to make you squirm."

On the ride home, I don't disagree with Dad's logic. I know he's right. But being the proverbial optimist, I'm confident Ashley's demeanor will change once we're married. Yes, I'm considering marriage again, and just to be safe, agree later with Mom to postpone that decision until the end of the school year.

• • •

After Thanksgiving break, back at Farleigh, Ashley and I get together to compare notes. I'm appalled when she confesses that Brad and his parents stayed in the same condo in Steamboat Springs with her and her parents. She must have noticed the expression on my face because she immediately swears it was an uncanny coincidence and that nothing happened with Brad. When I bite my lip and shake my head, she says, "I was with my parents the whole time and if I was trying to hide something, I wouldn't have told you about it in the first place."

I don't believe the coincidence is as innocent as she portrays. I think the whole thing was planned.

Several days later when I speak with Charlie, I tell him about Ashley, our reconciliation efforts, and the decision to put our contemplated marriage on hold. I appear to have alienated all my other sources for advice, and sadly enough, Charlie is still the only person I can really talk to.

"You're a glutton for punishment," Charlie says. "I know you're not asking for my advice, but I'm going to give it to you anyway. Don't!"

"Don't what?"

"Don't believe it was an 'uncanny coincidence' and don't paint yourself into a corner. To get married to Ashley would be like jumping out of an airplane without a parachute. You're going to be a crumpled mess when you land. Loving Ashley is like walking barefoot on broken glass. There's no way to escape getting cut to shreds."

Although I know both Charlie and my parents are right, I continue to pursue Ashley and enjoy the perks. I place the marriage proposal plan on hold and seriously consider discarding it altogether. Ashley and I maintain the *status quo*, and after Christmas comes and goes, Ashley finally takes the hint and our discussions of marriage cease. We both consider it a lost cause.

• • •

When I return from a recital midway through the second semester, I receive a telephone message from Ashley. She seems desperate.

"It's urgent that I speak with you ASAP! Call as soon as you receive this."

I'm perplexed and on high alert. *What could be causing Ashley so much distress?* I immediately return the call. "Where are you?" I ask.

"I'm in the lounge adjacent to the bookstore. Had to buy a book one of my professors recommended." Ashley pauses. I hear her sob. She continues, "Need to talk to you. Can you meet me here? I'm at the table next to the fireplace."

"Be there in five," I say, and close to panic, I grab my coat, gloves and hat.

When I arrive, it's obvious Ashley has been crying. I rearrange a chair so that we can speak without being overheard or without disturbing students who are poring over their studies.

"What is it?" I ask.

"Received a call from Dr. Benson's assistant. Appears I'm… pregnant."

"But I thought…" I blurt without finishing the sentence. I can feel my face flush. *Just remain calm*, I remind myself.

"Remember when I had those tests done?" Ashley asks.

"Yes, but I thought that was for something different."

"It was, but I was also concerned about having missed my period."

"Guess I didn't know." I put my arms around her to comfort her. I can see she's having a difficult time trying to control her emotions.

When I reassure her everything is going to be all right, the flood gates open and tears flow as never before. Fortunately, my handkerchief is clean, and I use it to help dry up the tears.

"I'm so sorry," she says several times in quick succession.

When I have a difficult time calming her, I say, "Guess our baby will need a daddy."

She manages a smile between sobs and asks, "Is that a…a proposal?"

"Usually, it's marriage first and then a family," I reply. "Why wait nine months?"

"Are you sure it's something you want to do?"

"The question is whether it's something *you* want to do."

"You know I've loved you from the day we met," she says when her emotions seem to have subsided somewhat.

"It seems as though we can't live with or without each other," I manage to say, still trying to stifle the shock.

"What's worse?" she asks.

"Living *without* each other." I say realizing I've just sealed the deal.

"Does that mean I get the ring back?"

"Two of them," I reply, "an engagement ring and a wedding band."

"Shouldn't you give this more thought? All of this is so sudden."

"I hadn't counted on a baby in the deal. It's like getting two for the price of one."

"I'm surprised at how well you're taking all this." Ashley has regained her composure. "It's not at all the reaction I expected. I thought about dropping out of sight for nine months and then reappearing. Glad I didn't have to."

I manage a smile. "The only difference between waiting to get married and just getting married is the lack of a waiting period. The shortest distance between two points is a straight line. Why take the long way when you can take a short cut?"

I consider Ashley's pregnancy a good omen; a sign from above. My vacillation gives way to a commitment I would no longer have to think about. The course is set and all I have to do now is follow it.

• • •

At spring break, we elope to Cancun. When we leave Mexico, Ashley is wearing the infamous engagement ring and the matching band. Two of our classmates had accompanied us on our jaunt to the spring break mecca. Justin Bowers served as my best man and his fiancée, Jessica Riggins, served as Ashley's maid of honor.

When I advise my parents of my plans to spend spring break in Cancun with Ashley, I don't tell them about the anticipated marriage nor Ashley's pregnancy. I fumble for the right words when Mom asks, "You're not keeping any secrets from us, are you?" Whether it was my guilty conscience or a mother's intuition, I sense Mom knows the score.

"Mom, you and Dad will be the first to know if that is the case," I reply.

Dad chuckles. "Don't forget the rings."

"I was a Boy Scout," I say. "I'm always prepared." Wasn't sure that was really the case but said it anyway.

. . .

The weekend after our return to Boston, Ashley moves in with me. I had rented a two-bedroom apartment when I returned to Farleigh thinking Charlie might be moving back to Boston. He stayed in New York. His decision proved to be a blessing as Ashley's belongings took up an inordinate amount of space. The garage has now been converted into a storage area to accommodate her precious belongings. Thank goodness, she didn't bring Maya, a likeable but rambunctious *bichon frisé*, with her. I was okay with expanding the family by two, but not three.

When I open the mail upon our return from Cancun, I field a letter from my mother. It had been mailed the day after I left with Ashley for Cancun.

> *Grady,*
> *Last night I had the most realistic dream I ever remember having. It was about the five of us, you, Ashley, Dad, me and the most adorable baby girl imaginable. Her name was Camey. It was as though we knew each other in another life. I was so startled and shaken, I even woke up your father. And you know how soundly he sleeps.*
>
> *Before we had you, I miscarried. The trauma has diminished little over these past years. The name your father and I agreed on when I found out I was pregnant with a girl was Camey. Yes, Camey, the name of the baby in my dream.*
>
> *When I told your father about the dream, he tried to analyze it. The only thing we can figure, in light of my sixth sense and your father's analytical mind, is that you and Ashley are going to have a baby. This explains your abrupt change of plans to reconcile and spend spring break with her in Cancun. I'm guessing by the time you two return you'll be married and have two*

announcements to make.

Before the dream, I would have been against a marriage your father and I thought ill-advised. Now, I'm of a different mind and would be delighted to have a daughter-in-law like Ashley and the Camey of my dreams.

Pardon the melodrama. My dream today is as vivid as it was last night. I pray that the dream will come true.

Love, Mom

• • •

When I call home, Dad says, "Hold on, son."

I hear Dad call Mom. Within a few seconds, she picks up an extension. "Graden, is that you?"

"Yes, Mom," I reply. "How are you doing?"

"Did you receive my letter?"

"I did."

"Well?"

Before I can respond, Dad asks, "Are congratulations in order?" This time he does not chuckle.

"Appears so," I manage to say amid a mix of emotions.

"I thought so," my mother says. "I pray both predictions are accurate."

"Affirmative as to both." I'm grateful for the reprieve and the affirmation I feared would not be forthcoming—at least not until I found the nerve.

"How far along is the new arrival?" Dad asks.

"Less than three months. It may be less than that."

After I hang up, I'm relieved my parents did not frown upon the pregnancy. Later, when I relay the good news to Ashley, she seems perplexed that I mentioned the pregnancy. It was then she made me promise not to mention it to *her* parents.

"They were shocked when we bypassed a formal wedding and

didn't invite the family," she says. "I don't want to cause any more distress."

It was okay to congratulate me for being a daddy but not okay to congratulate her parents for being grandparents. *Go figure!* When she notices the puzzled look on my face, she says, "They'll find out soon enough."

. . .

When I have a minute, I call and break the news to Charlie.

"It's now Mr. and Mrs. Graden Winslow," I say.

"I predicted as much!" Charlie says. "Why the rush?"

"Family expansion," I respond.

"A shotgun wedding?"

"You might call it that."

"I thought you wanted me to be your best man."

"Couldn't wait."

"When is junior due?"

"Sometime in October or November."

"Sure, the pregnancy isn't a ruse to get that proverbial ring through your nose?"

I'm surprised Charlie would accuse her of that. I'm fairly confident when I respond, "That's not something she would do." Then I vouch for her honesty, "Besides, I can verify it."

"Is she showing?"

"Not yet."

Charlie persists, "Have you talked to her doctor?"

"Not yet."

"Seen any reports?"

"No."

"Grady, what happens if you find out you've been duped?"

Charlie's attitude unmasks something smoldering deep within me, something I don't want to believe. I jump to the defense, "Won't happen. If I can't trust her now, how can I ever trust her?"

"And," Charlie retorts, "that's exactly my point. You forget, my friend. When could you ever trust her?"

Charlie's comment just adds credibility to my own doubts. I wallow in anguish and uncertainty, still walking barefoot on broken glass with no way out.

• • •

Near the end of the school year, I was asked to help direct a musical, *Brigadoon*. I would accompany the troupe to New York City and have an opportunity to visit my parents. Ashley was busy with a production of her own and preparing for finals and unable to make the trip.

During the return trip, Marles Minrish, a registered nurse and one of our neighbors, calls me.

"Grady, I hate to bother you but due to a fall, Ashley has had a miscarriage."

"Is she okay?"

"She was trying to negotiate the stairs with a load of books and apparently fell. Shortly after the fall, she started experiencing severe abdominal pains. She is resting at the moment and seems to be in shock."

"Is she in the hospital?" I ask, stunned by the news.

"She refused medical treatment and seems to be doing well on her own. If I thought it was necessary, I would have called for an ambulance. Appears she just needs rest and you to hold her hand."

"Marles, can you stay with her until I arrive?"

"Absolutely. Ashley said you were expected around ten p.m. That's less than three hours from now."

• • •

When I arrive, Ashley is sitting up in bed. Marles is sitting beside her telling her everything is going to be all right. I notice some blood splatters on the bedding as I rush to her side.

"I'm so sorry," Ashley sobs as I hold her close. "I so wanted the baby."

"I'll let the two of you be alone," Marles says as she starts for the bedroom door.

"Wait," I say as I catch up to Marles.

Outside, I ask what happened.

Marles finally says, "Early this morning, Ashley called me in a panic and told me about falling on the stairs. She said after the fall she began experiencing abdominal pain. She went to the bathroom, apparently had a miscarriage, and inadvertently flushed the immature fetus down the toilet. She was sobbing so violently I had difficulty understanding everything she was saying. I calmed her down and when I came in, the only remnants I saw were the blood stains on her underclothing." Marles pauses, and shakes her head, "Poor little thing asked that I get hold of you. That's when I called."

"Shouldn't we call a doctor?"

"I suggested that. Ashley became even more upset and was adamant about not doing so. She assured me she would be fine and only needed you. When a cousin of mine had a miscarriage early in her pregnancy, she didn't see a doctor. I told Ashley to see one in case any fetal tissue is still present in her womb. If there is any, it may pass out naturally. Or she can take medication or have the tissue surgically removed."

"Then she should see a doctor."

"Well, the risk of complications is very slight, and as adamant as she is about not having medical attention, it may do more harm than good to insist."

"I agree."

Marles gently pats my shoulder. "Wait seven to fourteen days to see if the tissue passes naturally. If the pain and bleeding have lessened or stopped in that length of time, that's a sign that the miscarriage has run its course and nothing else is necessary."

I breathe a sigh of relief at not having to insist Ashley seek medical attention immediately.

"You better get back in there," Marles says.

I look back at the bedroom door. Then I turn and say, "Thanks for being there for her and being such a good friend and neighbor. I... I..."

"Wouldn't have had it any other way. Just keep an eye on her and make sure she gets lots of rest. What she needs now is your reassurance that she is not to blame for the miscarriage and that you love her just the same. Now go on, get back in there."

I do just as Marles has suggested. With a little coaxing, I convince Ashley the miscarriage is not the end of the world.

"You don't think the pregnancy was just a hoax to get you to marry me, do you?" she asks.

"Shhh!" I say. "Even if that be the case, the end justifies the means. No pretext was necessary to get me to marry you. Only love is the answer."

Ashley grabs my hand and presses it to her cheek. Her tears trickle down between my fingers and I'm seeped in guilt for ever having doubted the pregnancy in the first place.

• • •

After Ashley receives her M.M. degree from Farleigh College of Music and I complete my contract, we travel abroad accompanying my father on still another concert tour. Alongside him, I became as much of a draw as he is. Occasionally, Ashley is involved, mainly to add variety and flair. She is an accomplished vocalist and a much-welcomed addition to Dad's team. She is also heavily involved in the administrative aspects of our musical performances. Her musical compositions are second to none and she makes a hefty sum on the side, writing and arranging music for several recognized performers, much like her grandfather before her.

When Ashley became pregnant with the twins, she decided she would like to move back to Colorado and away from the hustle and bustle of New York. Dad helped us buy a multimillion-dollar home on the Redlands overlooking Grand Junction. Dad put the house in a trust, which didn't set well with Ashley.

"Don't your parents think our marriage will last?" she asked at one point.

"I think Dad did it more for tax purposes and to protect the property from our creditors until we get on our feet," I said. "Eventually it will be put in our children's names."

Right after that, our twins, Shelly and Sherry, were born and they were named the beneficiaries of the trust. After Dad's attorney explained the rationale of a spend-thrift trust to Ashley, she accepted the arrangement but not without some choice expletives for my parents.

While the twins were growing up, our marriage journeyed over some bumpy roads, hit some snags, dead ends, detours, and of course, the usual twists and turns. However, for the most part, we pretty much rolled with the punches.

Once the twins hit college all of that changed. I was away a lot on concert tours. That left Ashley, as she described it, "orphaned and alone."

That insecure feeling I had when I courted her reared its ugly head, and I found myself drifting in a sea of rejection and it wasn't filled with salt water. Instead, I was drowning in a vodka-laden reservoir of despair.

Paranoia spelled the beginning of the end. My father and I were on a six-week tour in Canada, scheduled to perform at The Concert Hall in Toronto on Saturday, July 11, 2015. Ashley's fiftieth birthday was on Sunday the twelfth. To surprise her, I arranged to fly into Grand Junction early that morning. Instead of calling her, I took a taxi to our home. She wasn't there.

I showered and changed into slacks and a dress shirt, thinking we would celebrate Ashley's fiftieth when she got home. I had arrived with an expensive set of ruby earrings, and on the way, had stopped at a supermarket near the airport and picked up a dozen long-stemmed red roses. I had also made reservations for two at The Winery, one of Ashley's and my favorites, and across the street from the Avalon Theater where Ashley and I occasionally performed.

When midnight came and went, I started to worry. About 1:30 a.m., I heard someone opening the front door. The door banged against the wall. Boisterous laughter and the tinkle of glass as something hit and slid across the tile floor brought me on the run. When I turned on the hall light, it illuminated a tipsy Ashley and a man I readily identified as Brad Sessions. He was juggling an open bottle of wine and a glass in one hand and holding a key in the other. Ashley was carrying her purse in one hand and a fancy wrapped box in the other.

"What the hell!" I shouted. Brad didn't blanch but Ashley had a shocked look on her face and could only say, "What...what are you doing here?"

"I live here. What's *he* doing here?" I asked, pointing at Brad.

Still standing close to him, Ashley said, "He was on his way to Denver and stopped to help me celebrate my birthday. Since you weren't going to be here, I didn't think you'd mind."

If I had checked the garage when I got home to see if Ashley's car was there, I'd have known Ashley hadn't ventured out on her own and that someone likely had picked her up. I was not prepared for Brad. As I looked outside, I could see his Mercedes Benz glimmering in the moonlight. It did not look like it was poised for a quick getaway.

"Just happened to be in town and had remembered it was Ashley's birthday. Hope you don't mind me taking her out for dinner," Brad said in a slurred voice.

"Where are you staying?" I asked Brad.

"At the...Hadn't thought that far ahead," Brad stammered. "Where...ah...do you suggest?"

"Out near the airport." I pointed out the door.

Ashley shot me a go to hell look and turned to say her goodbyes to Brad. As they hugged and Brad left, Ashley turned to me and said, "Grady, it's not at all what you think."

"What do you think I think?" I asked.

"You know." Her eyes darted away, and she headed for the master bedroom.

...

I decided to give her the benefit of the doubt and handed Ashley her birthday gift. She appeared pleased with the earrings and immediately went to the bedroom mirror and tried them on. Then the moment turned awkward as I stood there waiting for her to open Brad's gift.

"Well?" I asked.

"Well, what!"

"Aren't you gonna open Brad's gift?"

"I'll do that later."

"Why not now?"

"Don't feel like it."

"Oh, but I insist."

"All right! Have it your way."

She then untied the bow and ripped the wrapping from the box exposing the Victoria Secret logo.

"There! Now, are you satisfied?"

"Open it!" I insisted.

"Open it yourself!" She flings the box in my direction. As she does so, the contents spill out onto the floor revealing a black gossamer negligee.

"Get the hell outta here," she screams as we both stare at Brad's gift.

That night I slept in the guest room upstairs.

...

The next day, on the pretext that I have an appointment with our accountant, I head to the law offices of Chevalier, Mills & Greenberg. With a little juggling of appointments, I'm able to meet with Adison Chevalier.

"To what do I owe this unexpected pleasure?" Mr. Chevalier extends his hand.

"Unfortunately, it's not a social call. I need a divorce and a discrete one at that. Also, I need an attorney who is firm but fair. I don't want to destroy my wife in the process. I love her too much for that. I just want to make sure I'm not taken for a ride."

"Are you saying the marriage isn't salvageable?"

My heart sinks and I'm embarrassed when I say, "I can no longer put up with her cheating."

He doesn't flinch. "What triggered the decision to proceed on a course of action of this magnitude?"

I tell him about Brad and Ashley and last night. He nods. "It appears you're convinced that your marriage is irretrievably broken meaning that it can't be mended. Am I correct?"

When I hear the words *irretrievably broken*, I cringe. "I tried to ignore the predictions of my family and a few close friends by turning a blind eye to Ashley's predilections. Despite the mounting evidence, I've been in denial."

"Did you know about the so-called 'predilections' before you married Ashley?"

I describe all the suspicious circumstances implicit in Ashley's behavior through our whole courtship. He just shakes his head and rests his chin on his fist. "Had a steady in law school for a short period of time that could have been Ashley's double," he says.

His admission makes me feel less like the fool I've painted myself to be. Apparently, I'm not such a freak after all. "I considered what happened before our marriage something my father referred to as sowing wild oats. I thought once Ashley and I were married, everything would be different. I didn't realize how delusional I really was. Guess love clouds all reason."

"Actually, what happened before marriage concerning infidelity is of little importance. And since Colorado has become a 'no-fault' divorce state, infidelity has little or no bearing for the most part."

I'm stunned. "You mean whether or not a spouse is unfaithful is irrelevant?"

"Credibility is always a factor and maybe in some fashion her deception, whether by lies or otherwise, might be deemed relevant.

Maybe you can expound on matters that occurred in regard to her infidelity following your marriage. Is that something you care to divulge?"

I run my hands through my hair. "Where do I start?" I ask more for my benefit than Mr. Chevalier's. Obviously, thinking the same thing, Mr. Chevalier does not respond.

"I really noticed her infidelity after our daughters left for college. At least, that's when the telltale signs started to appear."

"Do you remember the year they left for college?" Mr. Chevalier asks as he jots down notes on a yellow legal pad.

"Shelly and Sherry were born in 1990 and graduated high school at age eighteen. That would have been in 2008. In September of that year, they left for college."

"And the telltale signs?" Mr. Chevalier inquires, not looking up from his note taking.

I search my memory. "Ashley started losing interest in sex and seemed withdrawn. I thought it was part of the empty-nest syndrome. Then she would disappear without explanation. She spent more time at the mirror and hairdressers and expanded her wardrobe. She didn't answer the phone. She found excuses to be gone during the weekend. She began isolating herself. I became suspicious."

"Did you confront her with your suspicions?"

"She has a knack for making everything look like my fault. She would accuse me of hallucinating or being paranoid. It was the same when we were dating. She never would address the issue and would find ways to skirt around any accusation. She would admit to the circumstances but would deny any wrongdoing. She had a way of making me out the bad guy."

"Did she ever admit to being unfaithful?"

"Never. Accepting any kind of responsibility for her actions is not in her repertoire."

"Even when the cookie crumbs led in her direction?" Mr. Chevalier asks and looks up at me over the rim of his glasses.

"Especially then."

"Did you ever catch Ashley red-handed?"

I stifle the tears as I answer, "The closest was last night. Being with her former high school sweetheart, who lived in another state, on her fiftieth birthday, and me not expected back into the states for several more days is a smoking gun even for me."

"You don't think it was an innocent incident?"

"Do you?"

• • •

When I return home, Ashley is packing a suitcase.

"Where you going?" I ask.

"It's obvious I'm not wanted here." She didn't look up or interrupt her packing. "My parents have invited me to stay with them until the dust settles."

"Do we want to involve them?"

"Aren't they already involved?" She snaps. "They're not deaf, dumb and blind, you know?"

"What's that mean?" Anger rises in my gut.

"Come on, Grady. Don't you think they can see how your interest in being home has waned? Your preoccupation with your career, and of course the bottle, is not something you can easily hide."

"So, is that why Brad is back in the picture?" I lean my shoulder against the doorframe and fold my arms across my chest.

Ashley jerks her head up. Sarcasm drips when she replies, "Brad is my anchor. He's been a good friend, and unlike you, someone I can depend upon." She violently slams the suitcase closed. "Too bad I can't depend on you!"

True to form, whatever the issue, it's always my fault. I force myself to remain calm, and in a civil tone, ask, "Are you talking about your birthday?"

Ashley goes to the bathroom and gathers an assortment of cosmetics into an overnight case. She still refuses to look at me, "That's only one in a long list of examples. Your scheduling an out-of-country tour with your father on my fiftieth birthday speaks volumes about your priorities. How is it that I'm always the low man on the totem pole?"

"Well, you won't have me to kick around anymore. I'm filing for a divorce."

Ashley finally stops packing and glares at me, "I guess the spouse is always the last to know. Here I thought you came back because of my birthday. You can have these back." She throws the earrings at me, and I catch them both in mid-air. "If only you were as adept at sorting fact from fiction," she says and smirks.

"If it looks like a duck, walks like a duck and quacks like a duck, it probably is," I sputter, still struggling to maintain a grip on my anger.

No sooner had Ashley taken her bags to the car than she returned. She retrieves the negligee and waves it in the air. "At least someone appreciates me!"

• • •

Ashley is served with the petition for dissolution and responds by opposing the divorce and alleging the marriage is *not irretrievably broken* and attacking my competency because of *prolonged alcohol abuse*. She also requests that our residence be awarded to her and that I pay her alimony of five thousand dollars per month. It appears from her pleadings that she is being represented by Horace Shilling, an attorney from Gunnison who specializes in divorces. Fortunately, the twins are of legal age and emancipated, otherwise there would be a custody battle. A hearing is set on all contested matters, and I find myself once again opposing Ashley in court.

• • •

After I testify and establish that our marriage is *irretrievably broken*, I'm cross-examined by Shilling. He is scruffy and exudes arrogance.

"Is it okay if I call you Grady?" he asks.

"If you choose," I respond.

"You've been married to the Respondent now for over a quarter of a century. Am I right?"

"Yes." Mr. Chevalier had instructed me to just answer the question and not volunteer anything.

"You and Ashley have two grown daughters."

"Yes."

"And are proud of them?"

"Yes."

"Would you say you and Ashley were good parents and good role models?"

"Yes."

"Would it also be fair to say you and Ashley shared some of the same values, and throughout the marriage, had a partnership not just in name but in practice?"

"What do you mean?" Mr. Chevalier also instructed me not to guess at what a question might mean and not be afraid to ask for clarification.

"I mean during your marriage to Ashley, when the two of you raised your daughters and performed together in a musical group originally called Ashley and the New York Five, and later as Ashley and the GJs, you were a team."

"Yes."

"The two of you got along, I take it, both at home and on stage?"

"I'd say that was true, at least for the most part."

"I take it your answer is yes."

"Yes."

"Would it be a valid assumption on my part to say the petition for dissolution filed herein is the first either of you have filed?"

"Yes."

"So, for over twenty-five years, with the exception of a few bumps here and there as with most marriages, your married life was fairly stable?"

"Yes."

"Referring your attention to Ashley's fiftieth birthday, you were away on a concert tour with your father in Canada. Is that not true?"

"Yes."

"You led Ashley to believe you wouldn't be arriving back in the States until several days later. Am I correct?"

"Yes."

"In fact, it was your intention to surprise her on her birthday, wasn't it? And you succeeded in doing that, didn't you?"

"I certainly did!"

"When she arrived home with an old family friend with whom she was celebrating her birthday, you became upset. Right?"

"What husband wouldn't?"

"Just answer the question, Mr. Winslow," the judge admonished.

"Yes, I was upset."

"Was that the reason on the night of Ashley's fiftieth birthday, you chose to sleep in the guest room instead of with your wife and the reason you filed for divorce?"

"Among others."

"If you were to learn that the two were celebrating Ashley's birthday with Ashley's parents and that Brad Sessions' arrival was totally unexpected, would that still cause you to ask for a divorce?"

"If it was truly a coincidence that her old boyfriend just happened to be in town on her birthday, which I don't think it was, it would give me cause to at least pause. However, in light of their history together and their demeanor on their arrival from a night on the town, it would be a stretch to believe everything was on the up and up."

"Had you had anything to drink that night?"

"No, but it was obvious they did."

"You have a drinking problem. Is that not true?"

"If you say so."

"If Ashley says so, would she be wrong?"

"Probably not."

"If she says you are delusional, especially when you drink, would she also be wrong?"

"If she says so, then she's the one who's delusional."

"Judge, move to strike the answer as not being responsive."

"Overruled. I think he was responsive, Mr. Shilling."

"No further questions, Your Honor."

. . .

When Ashley testifies on direct, she is well rehearsed. She makes it appear that she is the victim of a crazed spouse who couldn't separate fact from fiction. She also makes it appear that on her own she would end up in the poor house; she neither had the means nor the capability to support herself. All she wants is to maintain the lifestyle to which she has been accustomed, especially in light of all the sacrifices she has made raising two daughters and having been married to me. All in all, Ashley's testimony is heartrending. That is until Mr. Chevalier begins his cross-examination.

"Mrs. Winslow, apparently Grady's assumption as to your intentions on the night of your fiftieth birthday was not as pointless and baseless as your attorney has painted?" The statement is posed in the form of a question.

"What exactly do you mean?"

"Tell the court which one of the following is not true: (1) Brad Sessions was the man who accompanied you home after your fiftieth birthday party at a time when your husband was expected to be out of town; (2) Brad Sessions was your ex-high school sweetheart; (3) Brad Sessions moved to Boston when you enrolled in school there; (4) you and Brad, and the only ones to do so, stayed behind for several days following a class reunion in Cancun after you started dating Grady; (5) when you and Grady broke off your engagement, you and Brad resurrected your relationship; (6) when you and Grady were re-engaged, you were still in a relationship with Brad; (7) when you moved back to Grand Junction, Brad closed his medical practice in Boston and relocated to Denver, a mere four hours from Grand Junction, (8) you continued to maintain a relationship with Brad during the whole time you were married to Grady; (9) on the night of your fiftieth birthday, you had Brad poised to stay at the home where you and Grady resided; and (10) Brad's gift to you on your fiftieth birthday was something one who, with established familiarity, would give another, to-wit: a flimsy nightgown."

"What evidence do you have that Brad and I maintained a relationship during the whole time I was married to Grady?"

"The witness is instructed to answer questions, not ask them," the judge admonishes. "Would you like to have the question repeated?"

"Yes, Your Honor!" Ashley replies.

"To simplify matters, let me approach it another way," Mr. Chevalier states as he resumes his cross-examination. "Is it fair to assume, that during the time you and Grady were married Grady did a fair amount of traveling around the world with his father, giving concerts of one form or another?"

"Yes."

"In other words, he was gone a good part of the time even when your twin daughters, Shelly and Sherry, were growing up. Correct?"

"Yes."

"In fact, your daughters referred to Brad as Uncle Brad is that not true?"

"That's supposition on your part!"

"Are you saying I'm delusional just like Grady?"

"It sounds like you might be."

"I take it you don't remember an incident that occurred when your daughters were in grade school and were shown your high school yearbooks, in the presence of both you and Grady, and when they spotted a picture of Brad Sessions, they exclaimed, 'There's Uncle Brad!'?"

"No, I don't remember that."

"You're not denying that occurred, only that you don't remember."

"Is that a question?"

"It is. Are you asking me to rephrase it?"

"Yes."

"Your twin daughters were familiar with your ex-boyfriend enough to recognize him and call him Uncle Brad. Am I correct?"

"If you say so."

"Mrs. Winslow, you're an accomplished woman and have worked throughout your entire marriage to Grady. Is that not true?"

"Not full-time."

"But that was at your choosing, especially while you were raising the twins who are now adults. Right?"

"Correct."

"You're still the lead singer in a group called Ashley and the GJs, if I'm not mistaken."

"Yes."

"You still have gigs on Friday and Saturday nights?"

"When I want."

"You're asking price is one thousand dollars a night, am I right?"

"We don't always get it."

"We're talking about just *your* share, right?"

"Yes."

"And you cut records or CDs and provide some of your songs to other artists for a price, correct?"

"Correct."

"And you hold a bachelor's degree as well as a master's degree in music? And the school you obtained both degrees was from Farleigh College of Music, or FCM?"

"Yes to both questions."

"You have requested to be allowed to remain in the residence on the Redlands?"

"Yes."

"Do you realize that the residence is in a revocable trust controlled by Grady's parents whereby your daughters are the beneficiaries subject only to a life estate?"

"Yes."

"Do you know who is listed as the life tenant?"

"Yes, Grady."

"So, you realize that it is not up to Grady whether you stay or don't stay in the residence?"

"Yes."

"Now, you're currently living with your parents here in Grand Junction?"

"Yes."

"And that the deed to your parent's home is a beneficiary deed and that you, as your parents' only heir, are listed as the beneficiary?"

"Yes."

"If Grady is allowed to live in the Redlands' residence and you continue to live with your parents on Quail Run, you'll both be residing in up-scale neighborhoods? Am I correct?"

"If you say so."

"One final question, Mrs. Winslow. If the roles were reversed and you were Grady, would you consider your lifestyle suspect or would you still insist that Grady was delusional."

"Appearances are deceiving, and Grady has never been able to separate fact from fiction."

"Ask your attorney if circumstantial evidence is just as good as eyewitness testimony and circumstantial evidence, in some cases, even more reliable."

"Objection," Shelling interposes. "Counsel is testifying and not the witness."

"Sustained," the judge rules.

"I'll withdraw the question," Mr. Chevalier announces.

• • •

Judge Clinton M. Grimes granted the divorce. Ashley was awarded no alimony and I'm still in the Redlands house. Ashley's only claim to fame is that her request to have her maiden name restored was granted. I can still remember telling Mr. Chevalier, at the end of his cross-examination of Ashley, "You nailed her to the wall with a velvet hammer."

Unlike our previous court case, when Ashley left the courtroom, she made a point of expressing her distain for Mr. Chevalier, Judge Grimes and me by shooting each of us an angry look that haunts me even to this day. Fortunately, it was not detected by Judge Grimes.

CHAPTER ELEVEN

Will We Ever Be Free From Each Other

GRADY

The divorce decree was like a presidential pardon. I felt as though an anchor had been removed from my neck. No more Ashley to contend with. No more desperation, no more recrimination, no more sleepless nights and no more escaping into a bottle. I didn't even celebrate my independence, at least not by drinking. My habit and all remnants of my habit were abandoned, and I experienced a relief that had eluded me at least during the second quarter century of my life. For the first time in a long time, I was looking forward to my next quarter or maybe even half century on this planet.

• • •

I scheduled my world concert tours with Dad and continued to compose music. I found myself writing church music and playing the piano and organ for the Episcopal church. Occasionally, I was asked to play for weddings and funerals for the three Catholic churches in Grand Junction. All in all, I was rather busy and had little time to dwell on the negative.

However, being alone so much, I couldn't help but obsess over Ashley's deceit and my foolishness. I was equally upset with Ashley's parents who wittingly or unwittingly facilitated the deception. Surely joining Brad and Ashley on her fiftieth meant they condoned the relationship. They, no doubt, were complicit in her love affair with Brad all along. It is also likely that they were against her breakup with Brad and her marriage to me all those years ago.   Although I resigned from our musical group, Ashley and the GJs, I would occasionally sub for the keyboard player and would find myself sharing the stage with Ashley. It bothered me more than it did her to hide our disdain for each other and fake infatuation, especially during our duets. Over a period of time, I began to shed much of the loathing and indifference I felt toward her. With the regular keyboard player being gone so much, I wondered if she might be orchestrating my increased involvement as a token of her remorse and a camouflaged peace offering.

I found that I rather looked forward to the gigs with Ashley and the GJs. Yet, I refused to let down my guard, and built an impregnable barrier that prevented even the thought of reconciliation from entering my mind, let alone my heart.

It had been six months since the divorce, and after a stunning performance at the Avalon, we found ourselves having a late dinner at our old haunt, The Winery. We were seated at our usual table in front of the fireplace.

"Seems like old times, doesn't it?" she remarks as she places her hand gently on my arm.

Watching the flames lick the artificial logs in hypnotic rhythm, and without looking at Ashley, I place my hand on hers. "Amazing the effect of an old flame."

Now, also mesmerized by the fluttering flames, Ashley replies, "I was thinking the same thing."

Realizing what I said and her reaction and not wanting to rekindle the old flame, I ease my hand away.

Ashley frowns and purses her lips. Then she says, "Will we ever be free from each other? Can we really say goodbye?"

When I don't respond, Ashley asks, "Have you already erased all those memories?"

"As hard as I try, I can't," I reply. "I can't close my eyes without thinking of the past—a time when there was just me and you."

"If you want to pen the lyrics," Ashley offers, "I'll start composing the music."

"Deal," I say already conjuring up a story line and a rhythmic flow of words. By the time we part and the two of us go our separate ways, I already have the lyrics to a new song. Obviously, it's entitled, ***Will We Ever Be Free From Each Other?***

Will we ever be free from each other?
Can we really say goodbye?
Now that we've parted and
Gone our separate ways
Will we look ahead and never back
To bygone days?
And when I give my love to another
Will I never think of the love
I gave to you?

Will we ever be free from each other?
Can we forget those tender years?
Can we close our eyes
Without thinking of the past
The day that I proposed and
The day you said I do?
Will we recall all the love that followed
And knowing our dreams came true?

Will we ever be free from each other?
Could we erase all those memories?
When we think of the love that we both have shared
Can we turn away and say we're glad
They've gone away?
And when you look back on your life
Will you think of the days
When there was just me and you?

Will you think of the days
When there was just me and you?

When I think back, the words were not just lyrics, they were the reflection of my soul.

It's easier to add music to words than words to music. When I present the lyrics to Ashley, she's delighted and conveys her joy with a kiss reminiscent of days bygone. For a moment I entertain that thought that got me in trouble the first time and almost every time since; but not this time. It's mind over matter. That inner voice that says "no" wins over its disappointed adversary.

Building a melody around the lyrics is truly a collaborative effort. When it comes to music, we're an effective and impressive combination in the mold of Rodgers and Hammerstein or maybe more like Sonny and Cher. We even surprise ourselves as to how quickly *Will We Ever Be Free From Each Other* comes together.

Rehearsal is a high and Ashley and I are putting the past behind us in an effort to make our new creation a hit. If the crowd reaction to the premiere of our new number is any indication, we're way off the charts. Following our gig at the Caravan, we celebrate with the bubbly—but not of the alcoholic variety. The bubbly is Ashley's charm and personality that makes her stand out brighter than any star in the heavens and makes her just as seductive as either Delilah or Cleopatra.

CHAPTER TWELVE

Can we Pick Up the Pieces

GRADY

It's difficult to be with Ashley and not feel that yearning. She seems impervious to the sting of the divorce and the cross-examination by my attorney that made her out the quintessential harlot. Yet, I continue to obsess over her breach of loyalty albeit less frequently as time passes.

Ashley's face in public and in front of our musical group surprisingly is the same one in private. If she harbors resentment, it doesn't show. In fact, it's just the opposite. She's not at all the hardened spurned spouse spawned by the rigors of divorce but the loving and compassionate Ashley I had fallen in love with a quarter century before.

After a late rehearsal, the sky is lit by a full moon that beckons from beyond. It's as if it were yesterday. We had both declined the invitation from our fellow musicians to join them afterwards for drinks. As Ashley and I walk together towards our respective vehicles, she grabs me by the arm and twirls me towards her. Our lips meet and by the magic of the moment, all the resentment, frustration and righteous indignation vanishes, leaving a vacuum that can only be filled with love. I'm not sure I want to make that grand leap.

We agree Ashley will accompany me home ostensibly to talk. On the veranda overlooking the lights of the city and a full view of the moon, we huddle together on the canopy swing we bought when we first moved to the Redlands. When the cool autumn air asserts itself, we move indoors. Ashley builds two hot chocolates topped with whipped cream and sprinkled with cinnamon and we sit in front of the fireplace with Ashley's arms looped through mine.

In the dimly lit room, shadows from the flames dance gracefully about the room. Ashley is the first to speak as she nuzzles close. "Would you agree that two of the most obstinate people on the face of this planet are in this room?" she asks.

"Certainly, the most stupid," I reply.

"It took a lot of effort on each of our parts to provoke the other."

"It worked."

"Do you really dislike me?" she asks.

"Just disappointed," I answer. "I'm sure I was a disappointment to you as well."

"I take the blame," she admits. "I deliberately went out of my way to get you to turn away. I guess my insecurity distorted my thinking and I figured that if you left me, it would be my doing and not yours. That way, it would be me who engineered the rejection."

Ashley taking the blame? "I don't get it," I say. "If you loved me, why would you want to hurt me?"

"Do you remember me saying years ago that when anyone got close to me, I had a compulsion to drive him or her away?"

"Yes, but—"

"Well, when I was a little girl, I had a kitten by the name of Cleo. I was crushed when the neighbor's dog got Cleo by the neck and tossed her around like a rag doll. I can still visualize that terrible scene. Even though the neighbor forced the dog to let go of Cleo, it was too late. That kitten was the first love of my life, and I was determined never to become attached to anyone or anything ever again. Even though my father brought home a replacement, I rejected it. I vowed never to be wittingly hurt again."

"That was beyond your control, not your fault."

"That's the point," she says. "Now you understand."

"Is that why you and Brad broke up?"

"I've never loved Brad. Because his parents and mine were neighbors and close friends and we were always together growing up, it was an arranged boyfriend-girlfriend relationship. I loathed Brad and always considered him a nerd. He was what even my parents called a fallback escort. Much of what I did later was just to make you jealous. The only man I've ever loved is you."

"If it's any consolation, I forgive you and ask that you forgive me. I still love you and always will. But I've built that same impregnable wall, and come hell or high water, no living being will come on this side again."

"That's too bad," Ashley says. "Hopefully, someday I can convince you to tear down that wall!"

• • •

Although I don't share everything with my parents, I do tell them all about my conversation with Ashley.

"That says a lot about Ashley," my father begins. "To admit what she admitted to and attempt to make amends speaks volumes."

"As the old adage goes," my mother says, "A leopard can't change its spots."

"Mom," I respond, "it's also an old adage that 'It takes two to *tango*' or is it 'It takes two to *tangle*?' The breakup wasn't all Ashley's fault. I'm not perfect, you know."

"For the two of you to bury the hatchet would obviously be best for the twins," my mother says. "I'm sure they love you both. At least you're still together—professionally speaking. If it's more than that, you're acting at your peril."

"Lightning doesn't strike twice," my father adds. "Grady has a good head on his shoulders and is fully capable of making wise decisions. Let him be."

"If we didn't love you, we wouldn't be so concerned," Mom says. "Don't be taken in by Ashley's broken promises. Broken promises lead to broken hearts."

• • •

After I switch off my cell, I'm curious about the origin regarding the leopard not changing its spots. When I Google it, I'm surprised to find it's in the Bible. When I go to check, I also read the passage in Genesis where Eve eats of the forbidden fruit in the Garden of Eden and offers the same to Adam. It always intrigued me that Adam allowed himself to be tempted, contrary to his better judgment. It occurred to me that I was doing much the same when it came to Ashley. Against my better judgment, I let my guard down and allowed her to convince me otherwise. It seems I'm powerless to resist—much like Adam must have been all those centuries ago. *Things haven't changed much.*

• • •

Although we don't haggle, Ashley makes it known that even though legally our marriage is irretrievably broken, in reality it's not. Her rationale is that since we both still love each other, we should give it another try. I wonder whether we can ever pick up the pieces and put them back together. I've always been able to think better when I'm sitting at the piano. When I do, I find myself composing still another song for Ashley. It's called, ***Can We Pick Up the Pieces*** and the lyrics go something like this:

> Can we pick up the pieces and
> Put it back together?
> Is there any reason to really try?
> Can we pick up the pieces all scattered
> Without thinking of things that made us cry?
> Will we find it in our mind and heart
> To come up with a reason
> We should make a brand new start?

> Can we pick up the pieces and
> Put it back together?
> Is there any reason to really try?
> Can we pick up the pieces without missing a few?
> Could we live happily together as we promised
> we'd do?

Can we set aside all our hurts and fears
Or will tomorrow be like yesterday
Bringing more tears?

Can we pick up the pieces and
Put it back together?
Is there any reason to really try?
Can we pick up the pieces each little bit
Not knowing in advance
Whether any may fit?
Have we really changed our thoughts and ways
Or have we built impossible dreams
On impossible days?

CHAPTER THIRTEEN

The Defining Moment

GRADY

It's now Christmas time and Ashley and I are sitting by the fireplace in my Redlands home. The fire in the fireplace and the lights from the tree I put up are the only illuminations in the room. I take her hand and ask her what she would like for Christmas.

"You know" she says, as she snuggles next to me.

"What?" I ask even though I suspect what her response will be. "You know I love you," I respond. "But I can't make a commitment at this time unless there are conditions attached."

"Like what?" Ashley asks, obviously perturbed.

"Like you won't leave me stranded again. When you're through with me for the moment, you cast me aside like an outdated pair of shoes."

"I can't predict the future, and like you, can't make a commitment I can't absolutely guarantee," she replies.

"Precisely my point! Neither of us can make a commitment we can't absolutely keep."

"Grady, you're hopeless!" She jerks her hand out of my grasp and moves away from me. "Heaven knows I've tried to make amends and be the person you want me to be."

I struggle to keep from saying something I might regret. *When did she ever put my feelings before her desires?* If it weren't so pathetic, I'd laugh.

Apparently oblivious to her skewed view of the past, she goes on, "I'm unwilling to continue to be the lady in waiting—waiting for you to make up your mind. Time doesn't wait and neither will I. You have my cell number. Call me if you change your mind. In the interim, I'll be pursuing other possibilities."

She says that like it's something new in her life. I help her on with her coat and see her to the door. "Drive safely," I say as she stomps her way through the snow to her car. Something tells me all the stomping isn't related to the accumulation of snow.

At a rehearsal several days later, Ashley announces she has a new song.

"What's its title?" our drummer asks.

"*The Defining Moment*," she says. Requisitioning my keyboard and turning on the mic, she plays a short intro and then begins to sing:

> I'm in a quandary thinking of you
> Trying to forget is like trying to smile
> Both elude me since you left
> The day we met was a defining moment
>
> My love is on hold waiting for you
> I've got to know which way to go
> If you do come back it might be too late
> Life may bring me another defining moment
>
> The suspense was too much, too much to bear
> Found someone to care, my destiny to share
> No more uncertainty in gambling on you
> I've since discovered the defining moment

When her song ends and after our applause subsides, Ashley comes over to where I'm standing and kisses me full on the lips. "Grady, I will always love you. Have a nice life without me." She turns and leaves the room. It would be months before I would see her again. And when I do, she's with Brad.

CHAPTER FOURTEEN

Turn Back to Me

GRADY

I was the lone dissenter when Ashley was asked to rejoin the GJs. I had no idea where Ashley had been the past three years. No one asked and Ashley didn't say. Ashley and I, for the most part, were civil toward each other. Other than professionally, we had little contact with each other—which seemed to suit us both.

It's at the Caravan and on my birthday that Ashley announces she has written a new song for me. I found out later, the rest of the band was in on the surprise.

"This song was written by me as a tribute to Grady Winslow, our keyboard player and my inspiration and my former husband," Ashley announces to the audience. It's entitled ***Turn Back To Me***. I listen intently as she sings:

> *Turn back to me*
> *You've touched my heart*
> *Turn back to me*
> *Can't be apart*
> *Turn back to me*
> *I love you so*
> *Turn back to me*
> *You're all I know*

> I don't deserve a second chance
> A second chance at love
> Don't deserve a second glance
> A second glance from you

I know I have a lot of love
A lot of love for you
Now I'm chasing an elusive dream
A dream you could make come true

Turn back to me
You've touched my heart
Turn back to me
Can't be apart
Turn back to me
I love you so
Turn back to me
You're all I know

My heart was settled long ago
A time we both were young
Didn't know it at the time
You were the only one
I was different when I left
But now I'm not the same
Give me a chance to prove my love
I'll not be happy 'till you do

Turn back to me
You've touched my heart
Turn back to me
Can't be apart
Turn back to me
I love you so
Turn back to me
You're all I know

It's unwise to chase a rainbow
But chase and chase I must
Each time I dream of happiness

I dream of the two of us
The only fond recall I have
Are days I spent with you
Those thoughts are now what move me
And keep me turning back to you

Turn back to me
You've touched my heart
Turn back to me
Can't be apart
Turn back to me
I love you so
Turn back to me
You're all I know

The music fades, and with the mic still in her hand, she raises her eyebrows and with that special look that was all her own, says, "Well?"

"Tomorrow!" I reply. Her overture is tempting but I don't succumb—at least not then.

"Don't give me tomorrow...tomorrow may never come!" she says, and the look in her eyes tells me she can predict the future.

July fifteenth is just another bright, sunny day in Grand Junction. At 9:00 a.m., the temperature is already well into the seventies with the high expected to be in the nineties by midafternoon. The hum of the air conditioner is a welcome distraction. Adison Chevalier had already loosened his tie and unbuttoned the top button of his shirt.

Adison usually was at the office by 7:30 a.m. if he was not in trial and earlier if he was. Verna, his secretary of many years, was the one who kept him on track and provided him with his morning coffee, a fresh pastry and a printout of his scheduled appointments and reminders for the day. Attached to a stack of client files were typed pleadings and correspondence requiring his signature.

Included in the stack this day was an envelope addressed to Ashley Harden with the following notation scribbled on it:

> ***Mr. Chevalier, please provide this in person to Ashley no earlier and no later than July 15, 2015. Have her remove the contents in your presence to confirm delivery. Bill me.***
>
> ***Grady Winslow***

On the envelope was Ashley's telephone number in the same handwriting. "Hmmm," Adison said to himself as he punched the intercom. "Verna, bring me the Winslow divorce file!"

Within minutes, Verna appeared and handed Adison an accordion folder bulging with letter-sized and some legal-sized segregated folders and envelopes.

"Do you know what this is all about?" Adison asked Verna, waving the sealed envelope addressed to Ashley with Grady's written instructions and the firm's intake stamp showing the date of

January 16, 2015.

"I have no idea," Verna said after examining the envelope. "Must be pretty important considering we haven't heard from Mr. Winslow in quite some time."

"Last time I talked to him was about six months ago. The conversation was strange. He wanted to make sure I had received the envelope he had left with Thelma and to confirm the length of time the winner of the PowerBall jackpot had to claim the prize." Adison rubbed his chin as he reflected on that day some six months ago. "He's one of our regular clients and perhaps one of our most *conscientious*, if you know what I mean," Adison said, winking and pulling out his wallet and pointing to it. "Schedule an appointment with Ashley. Grady's instructions say to schedule it for today. Time appears to be of the essence."

When Verna phoned Ashley requesting she come in for a short appointment with Mr. Chevalier, Ashley told her that was pretty short notice and that she was "much too busy to drop everything to come in today." Even when Verna said it might be very important, Ashley bristled and snarled "If it has to do with Grady, what on earth can be that important?" So, Ashley's appointment was scheduled for the following Monday, July twentieth.

• • •

"Hope you don't mind if Brad accompanies me?" Ashley asks, as she enters Adison's office with Brad on her heels.

"Heavens no," Adison replies, as he stands and extends his hand.

"I don't think you've met my new husband, Brad Sessions," she says, urging Brad forward. "This is Grady's attorney, Adison Chevalier." Brad and Adison shake hands.

Adison hands Ashley the envelope and says, "Grady wanted you to have this."

"What's in it?" Ashley asks as she grabs the envelope. It's obvious she still has little tolerance for anything to do with Grady. Using her index finger, she carelessly tares back the flap.

A lottery ticket flutters to the floor. When Brad bends and picks it up, Ashley snatches it from him.

"This is what you brought me in here for? It's just a lottery ticket!" Ashley snaps as she glares at the ticket and then at Adison. She looks into the envelope again. She takes out the enclosed page from the six-month old newspaper and unfolds it. She stares at the page with the winning PowerBall numbers and compares them against the lottery ticket she's holding in her hand. Out loud, she reads, "01-01, 05-05, 08-08, 12-12, 19-19...PB 25-25." Her eyes grow wide as she stares open-mouthed at the two items.

"Oh, my God," she blurts and waves the winning lottery ticket in the air. She repeats over and over, "I'm a billionaire, I'm a billionaire."

Brad is straining to compare the numbers. He wrestles the winning ticket out of Ashley's hands. Not wanting to risk tearing the ticket, Ashley reluctantly releases her hold and Brad compares the numbers. Within seconds, Brad and Ashley are locked in each other's arms dancing wildly around Adison's desk.

While Ashley and Brad perform their victory dance, Adison examines the page from the newspaper. The newspaper was dated January 15, 2015. The six-month or 180-day redemption period began on that date, the day after the drawing. Adison looks at his calendar. *Today's date is July 20, 2015, five days later than the day we tried to schedule the appointment with Ashley and the day we were instructed by Grady to contact her. Oh, my God! The redemption period expired five days ago!*

Ashley jerks the paper from Adison's hands and says, "Eat your heart out, Chevalier. Too bad you didn't represent me." She thumbs her nose at Adison. "This is for your cross-examination of me at the divorce hearing." With the newspaper and the lottery ticket, she and Brad stroll out of Adison's office, down the corridor, through the reception area, out the double doors and onto the street.

• • •

Adison rears back in his worn leather swivel chair and entwines his fingers across his ample girth. He knew she'd be livid. He can hardly contain his joy as he reflects on one of life's little ironies which is about to unfold before his very eyes. Within minutes, Ashley storms back into his office with Brad and Thelma on her heels. Before Thelma can apologize for the intrusion, Ashley is already inside Adison's office.

She screams, "Chevalier, you rotten, conniving, miserable son-of-a-bitch. Whatta a cruel sick joke! You and your worthless client set me up!"

"Now, hold on! If you'd come in when we tried to schedule you, you'd…"

"Hold on, nothing! How in the hell did Grady forge the lottery ticket? He's not smart enough to have done it on his own! As his brain and mouthpiece, you're probably the one responsible for all of this!"

"You didn't let me finish my sentence."

"Sentence, hell! I'll have your license for this!"

As Ashley clinches her fists and moves toward Adison, Brad grabs her. "Calm down, honey! Let's listen to what he has to say."

Brushing Brad aside, she folds her arms and glares at Adison. "Okay, spill it! What do you have to say for yourself?"

"It's no joke! If you'd come in on the date we requested, you'd be one point five billion dollars richer."

"You expect me to believe you?"

"Don't take my word for it. Check with the Grand Junction branch of the State Lottery Office. It's just down the street. If you don't know where it is, Thelma will provide you with the address."

"Don't bother. We'll find it on our own."

The two retrace their steps out of Adison's office, down the corridor, through the reception area, out the double doors and back out onto the street.

• • •

"I hate to bother you, Mr. Chevalier, but we have an irate Ashley Sessions holding on the line demanding to speak to you. She says she's calling from the lottery office."

"Tell her I've left for lunch and a golf date with Grady at the country club."

"But…" Thelma says, "you don't play golf and you have appointments in the office all afternoon."

"Never mind that. Just tell her what I said. That way she'll know I hadn't bet on the wrong horse after all."

Soon Thelma is back on the intercom. "Not everything Mrs. Sessions said can be repeated. However, she accused you and Mr. Winslow of collusion and said that what the two of you did was an unforgivable sin. She said the two of you should rot in hell."

"Sour grapes!" Adison replies.

"But…" Thelma fumbles.

"But what?" Adison asks.

"But…Mrs. Sessions said, just before she hung up, that she could understand how Mr. Winslow could cut off his nose to spite his face even to the tune of one point five billion dollars but said, 'As devious and mercenary as his attorney is, his attorney would have opted for the dough-re-me.'"

"Yes?"

"She said she wasn't so sure of what she just said about you was true and added that you were probably the one who advised Mr. Winslow, in the quest for retribution, to trade one point five billion dollars for vindication."

He chuckles. *Grady, you old dog, you get the last laugh after all.* Then Adison says, "*Purely circumstantial*, Thelma. *Purely circumstantial!*"

GRADY

After Mr. Chevalier called and told me what happened when Ashley and Brad appeared in his office, I suddenly remembered Ashley's words to me the night we performed at the Caravan. After she sang *Turn Back to Me,* she looked at me and asked, "Well?" I remember responding, "Tomorrow." Ashley's reply was "Don't give me tomorrow…tomorrow may never come!"

Sadly enough, her prediction has proven to be accurate. There are no more tomorrows for Ashley and me. Too much water has passed under the bridge, and now alone in my studio, as always, I turn to music to express my emotions. Having resigned myself to the truth of our situation, I begin to compose a number that chronicles our relationship. I entitle it ***Brokenhearted***:

> *You're the one I want, but you don't want me*
> *So brokenheartedly I set you free*

> I'm controlled like a puppet on a string
> Without you, my love, life don't mean a thing
> So as much as I want you in my life
> Your wandering ways will always cause strife

> *You're the one I want, but you don't want me*
> *So brokenheartedly I set you free*

> When you told me you've got to be you
> I didn't know that it meant you'd be untrue
> You lied to me without saying a word
> I can't ignore all the rumors I've heard

> *You're the one I want, but you don't want me*
> *So brokenheartedly I set you free*

> As much as I crave the joy that you bring
> Not going to be that puppet on a string
> We've both paid the price for love gone bad
> My heart still longs for the life we once had

> *You're the one I want, but you don't want me*
> *So brokenheartedly I set you free*

A billion dollars can't ease the pain
Memories of you will always remain
I know you can't see a future with me
Now I have no choice but to set us free

You're the one I want, but you don't want me
So brokenheartedly I set you free

As it turned out, Grady had one more song to sing. It was entitled *You, Me And The Lottery.*

> *Lady Luck smiled down on me*
> *I just won the lottery*
> *How many tickets did I buy*
> *Don't know, can't count that high*
> *Was it luck or did I try*
>
> *Odds were 1 in 25*
> *To win a prize of any size*
> *Five balls numbered 1 to 69*
> *Heavenly stars were in align*
> *Good guess; the money was mine*
>
> *Even with all the tickets sold*
> *My predictions were all foretold*
> *Six letters in ASHLEY's name*
> *Matching numbers in the alphabet*
> *Those I used to place my bet*
>
> *Lady Luck smiled down on me*
> *I just won the lottery*
> *It did little to win Ashley's heart*
> *As of yet we're still apart*
> *It's now just me and the lottery*

You, Me and the Lottery

Carroll Multz

The Winning Ticket

SONG LIST

About the Author

CARROLL MULTZ, a trial lawyer for over forty years, a former city attorney, two-term district attorney, assistant attorney general, United States Commissioner, and judge, has been involved in cases ranging from municipal courts to and including the United States Supreme Court. His high-profile cases have been reported in the **New York Times**, **Redbook Magazine** and various police magazines. He was one of the attorneys in the **Columbine Copycat Case** that occurred in Fort Collins, Colorado, in 2001 that was featured by Barbara Walters on **ABC's 20/20**. He recently retired as an Adjunct Professor at Colorado Mesa University in Grand Junction, Colorado, where he taught law-related courses at both the graduate and undergraduate levels for twenty-eight years. In addition to the ten novels in **The Childhood Legends Series**®, he has authored or co-authored thirty-three adult novels and eight books of nonfiction including his recently released handbook entitled **Testifying in Court—A Guide for Peace Officers**.